YOURS TO KEEP

LANTERN BAY, BOOK 4

SOPHIE HAYDON

BAY BOOKS

Yours to Keep
by Sophie Haydon

An open-hearted hippy, a secretive property tycoon—a recipe for heartache. Amber Connelly is adored by her family for her sunny, quirky personality. So what is she doing, her family wonders, lusting after a straight-laced property billionaire?

—The Mackenzies—
A Place Called Home
Secrets at Parata Bay
Escape to Shelter Springs
What you See in the Stars
Second Chance at Whisper Creek
Summer at the Lakehouse Café

—Lantern Bay—
Yours to Give
Yours to Treasure
Yours to Cherish
Yours to Keep
Yours Forever
Yours to Love

For more information about this author, visit:
https://sophiehaydon.com

ISBN: 978-0-9951447-6-7 (epub)
ISBN: 978-1-9910211-6-8 (2022 Amazon Print Edn)
ISBN: 978-1-9910213-3-5 (2022 Draft2Digital Print Edn)

CONTENTS

"The lamp burns bright when wick and oil are clean."
— **Ovid**

---

*D*avid Tremayne slammed shut the door to his car and looked over its roof toward the café. There she was. He smiled to himself as he watched her fuss over one of her elderly customers, helping them to the door and giving them a gentle hug before they went on their way. He could practically feel the glow of happiness emanating from the old lady as she walked slowly away towards the waiting taxi. She seemed to have that effect on everyone.

He paused a moment to admire the waitress's slender figure as she jumped up to reach something from a high shelf. He sighed. A big heart and a beautiful figure. What more could a man want?

He walked across to the café and his smile broadened at the sight of her cooing over a small baby. As he paused by the window, she looked up and his breath caught. He looked away abruptly and for a brief moment noticed his reflection, revealed by a poster in the window, and not for the first time was surprised at his contained, buttoned-up appearance. There was no hint of the smile he could have sworn he'd worn, no sign his heartbeat had quickened at the sight of her, no evidence he was in danger of falling for a woman because of the size of her heart.

But he wouldn't, because he needed her. Without her support, his project would be doomed before it had begun and he couldn't afford any more adverse publicity. No, there would be no falling for the beautiful woman with the big heart. He only needed her for a while and then he'd let her go. Seduce and discard. How hard could that be?

He pushed the door open, the bell jangled, and he stepped inside the café.

AMBER CONNELLY LOOKED up as the café bell jingled. She didn't do it every time—that would have been plain crazy as the café was a busy place—no, only at five minutes past one every day, except for weekends.

She watched the tall, broad-shouldered man in the business suit—the only suited person in the café—walk past her without looking at her and take a seat by the window. He picked up a menu and studied it. Why, she didn't know. He must have known its contents by now. And besides, he always chose the same thing.

She was about to collect her pen and paper as the door opened again and Gabe and Maddy entered, laughing and holding hands. She grinned to see her brother and sister-in-law so happy. The suited man raised an eyebrow at the noise, as if irritated by the distraction, before returning to peruse the menu. As Gabe walked by, he caught the eye of the man and Amber could sense a bristling—Gabe being protective, as usual.

Amber waved them to their usual table and walked up to the man. He was aware of her presence—she knew that even though he didn't look up. She smiled to herself. He really intrigued her, even though he wasn't anything like the type of guy she was usually interested in.

She smiled. "Good morning. How are you today?"

He looked up, and as usual, her heart nearly stopped. Surely it was indecent for a man to be endowed with such beautiful green eyes. "It's afternoon," he said.

"Oh! So it is," she said, unable to focus on anything but those eyes.

"It's past twelve, which is the middle of the day, so it's afternoon. You were incorrect," he added for good measure, as if she doubted his words. She didn't. She only ever doubted herself. Everyone else—especially this man who she imagined would be incapable of error—she always accepted as being correct.

She grinned, and his eyes narrowed.

She chuckled at his response and he frowned.

She laughed out loud—he must be the straightest, most pedantic man she'd ever met—and he looked away, back at the menu, his frown deepening. She felt the brightness fade from the day as he turned his eyes away. She wanted them looking at her again.

"You're right! Of course it's afternoon. I should know, we're serving lunch." She ducked her head so he couldn't hide from her gaze. "So what's it to be?"

She was rewarded with another look from those green eyes, their composure once more intact. He handed her the menu. "Caesar salad with chicken. Keep the dressing to one side. Are the wholemeal rolls fresh?"

"Fresh?" Amber repeated the last word, hoping it would help her concentrate on what he was saying.

"Yes. The rolls. Are they fresh? I only want them if they've been freshly made today."

Jeez, he was one out of the box. "Everything's fresh. The bread was made this morning with my own fair hands."

Those green eyes slid down to her hands and she suddenly felt self-conscious about the ring she was wearing. She wasn't supposed to wear rings but must have forgotten to slip off the greenstone and silver ring she'd inherited from her mother.

"When I said 'fair' hands," she began to blather, trying to slide the ring around and hide her hands under the notebook on which she was taking his order, "I meant, you know, reliable hands. Because they're not that fair. Not really."

"In what way are they 'not fair'? They look perfectly fair to me. Well formed, and…" He hesitated, uncharacteristically. "Quite attractive."

"Oh!" The single word slid out on a sigh. She wasn't smiling any longer. Instead the curious low-key fizzing in her stomach she experienced whenever she saw him, stepped up a notch. "Thank you." She held up her hand. "Yes, I suppose they're not bad, are they?"

"No. So if you agree, what did you mean by they're not fair?"

"Oh, that." She shrugged and wrinkled her nose self-deprecatingly. "I just mean that I'm not that good a cook. Enthusiastic but by all accounts—well, by my family's accounts—not actually that good."

"And yet you've made the bread rolls. You're not doing a good job at selling them to me."

"I'm good at rolls. Anything with yeast is okay because I can give it a bit of a bash. Heavy handed, you see?" she said, slamming her hand on the table. Everyone looked around but the man himself didn't move an inch. Instead he touched her ring, accidentally brushing the back of her hand as he did so.

"Heavy hands, maybe." He looked back with eyes that had dropped the facade and made her melt deep inside. "But they're beautiful ones."

She took an involuntary step back, wondering if she'd heard right. This was the rude guy, yes? Not someone who flattered. She didn't reply and turned abruptly.

"Excuse me!" he called after her. She stopped in her tracks, and turned slowly, wondering what on earth he was going to say. Was he about to tell her he was wrong, her hands weren't in the slightest bit beautiful, or maybe that he didn't want his lunch after all? Maybe she'd dreamed the whole thing.

"Yes?" she asked breathlessly.

"And a coffee, please. Short black."

"Right," she said, more to herself than to him. "Right. Coffee it is." Coffee it was every day. If there was one thing that the green-eyed man who made her legs go weak was, it was predictable. But, as she walked over to her brother's table, she considered the word. Predictable was a bit negative. Maybe regular, or 'knows what he wants' would be more accurate. Yes, that was infinitely better. Because he'd just turned out to be anything but predictable.

She brought out her notebook and poised her pen but her mind was full of the word 'beautiful'. She turned the hand that was holding the notebook and studied it.

"What the hell are you doing, Amber?" asked Gabe. "Is there something wrong with your arm? Here"—he reached out in his best doctorly fashion—"let me take a look."

She snapped back to the present and pulled her arm from Gabe's hand. "No. Of course not." She shook her head, trying to rid herself of the sensation on the back of her hand from where the green-eyed man had touched her, trying to focus on the present. It wasn't easy—her family had always accused her of having only a weak grip on reality. She took it as a compliment.

"Then why do you look so goofy?"

Now that annoyed her. Goofy was the last thing she wanted to look at that precise moment. She glanced at the man but he was flicking away an annoying wasp from his table.

"Amber! You haven't taken our order," said Gabe.

She dismissed him with a wave of the hand. "In a minute." She returned to Green Eyes' table, leaned over and opened a window. With the aid of a menu, she carefully scooped up the wasp and flicked it gently out of the window. She pulled the window closed once more. She turned to see that he was completely still, his eyes focused intently on her.

"I'll leave it closed." She mimed a shiver. "It's a bit chilly outside this... *afternoon*." She grinned at the added emphasis.

He cleared his throat and sat up straight. "You should have one of those fly things to kill flies and wasps. They're pests."

Her grin faded. "They're *not*. I'm not into killing things, and we usually have the windows open so things fly in, and then they fly right on out again." She looked around defensively. "Anyway, do you see any flies?"

He cast a steady look around and pointed into a distant corner by the open front door. "There."

"That's not fair. That one's just come in." She pointed. "And look, it's just gone out again."

He shrugged.

"And what does that shrug mean?"

"Simply that I proved my point."

"You did no such thing. Anyway, if you don't like it, there *are* other cafés."

He held her gaze for a long moment and she felt her irritation wobble and then flutter and dissolve into nothing, like a popped sigh, or a rain cloud evaporating under a hot sun. He might not be able to talk without provoking her but he sure could speak with those eyes, and she liked what they were saying. A loud ding sounded from across the café.

"I don't want to go to other cafés because they don't have you as a waitress."

A small whimper escaped her lips and she touched her burning cheek. She never blushed—what on earth was happening?

The ding sang out again.

"Someone at the counter is trying to attract your attention." He glanced across the café. "Yes, two lattes by the look of it." He frowned. "Funny color, must be soy or something strange."

She nodded and stepped back. "Right, I…" She turned and walked away, waving her hand as Gabe tried to attract her attention again. Once the two lattes had been deposited—and how the green-eyed stranger knew soy milk had been used, she had no idea—she went to take Gabe and Maddy's order.

"What's got into you, Amber? You're acting all distracted. Well, even more distracted than usual."

Amber pressed her hand flat against her chest, willing her heart to stop pounding, willing the heat that she could feel flooding her cheeks to subside.

"Are you having a panic attack?"

She took a deep breath and shook her head. "No," she said, "I'm just…" She shrugged. "I don't know what I'm just doing." She flashed what she hoped was a reassuring smile at her big brother. "Now, what's it to be, the same as usual?"

She glanced across at the green-eyed man once more. She couldn't seem to stop herself. Gabe followed her gaze and frowned. "That guy's been here every day this week."

"Yeah," agreed Amber. "And last week. You probably didn't notice him last week."

Gabe's gaze narrowed as he turned to her. "Who is he?"

She shrugged. "No idea. He's the guy who we saw running that time. You know, the guy I asked you to check out. But you didn't, so I don't know who he is."

"I can't go checking out every guy you fancy. For one thing, there's too many, and for another it would look weird."

Amber tutted. "So, thanks to you, I have no idea who he is."

Gabe shook his head, defeated.

"He sure is hot," murmured Maddy.

Gabe shot an indignant look at Maddy before glancing angrily at Green Eyes.

"So, have you got past the small talk yet?" Maddy asked, ignoring Gabe's frowning glare.

Gabe looked from Maddy back to Amber, then back to Maddy again. "Small talk," grunted Gabe. "Why would you want to bother?"

"Because he's hot," Amber and Maddy said together. It didn't improve Gabe's mood.

"I don't think so."

Amber and Maddy exchanged amused looks and Maddy leaned over and kissed Gabe. "That's because you're a man."

"You women don't know everything," he said, a smile once more back on his face.

Maddy rolled her eyes. "Just because you're the town's GP doesn't mean you know *everything*."

"And in this case," continued Amber, "you definitely don't." She paused for dramatic effect. It worked. Gabe's mouth hung open slightly as if he had no idea what she was about to say. Amber liked that. She rarely had any of her family guessing. "He's going to ask me out."

"He's what?" Gabe shot the stranger another look. "Has he been chatting you up?"

"No," she said, trying to make herself heard above a noisy crowd who were just leaving the café. "Well, not unless you call asking me if the bread is freshly baked, or whether we use virgin or extra virgin—"

"Virgin?" Gabe raised his voice over the shouts of the departing diners. "He asked you if you're a virgin?" Gabe stood up, but Maddy pulled his arm, and Amber squeaked with embarrassment.

"No, stupid brother, he didn't. He wanted to know about the oil."

"Oil? Maddy, tell me what she's talking about."

"Gabe," said Maddy. "That guy over there has the hots for Amber and we've laid bets on when he'll ask her out. I've lost already. I said yesterday. But Amber reckoned he's going to wait seven days before asking. Apparently he's some kind of accountant or something and does everything in sevens."

Gabe looked at Amber incredulously. "An accountant? Really, Amber? Since when have you ever dated anyone who *could* count, let alone wear a suit."

"Don't be so damned rude. Astro could count. He had a steady beat going when he was playing the drums. Anyway, give me your order, I've got work to do."

She walked past Green Eyes, pausing to give an adjoining table an unnecessary wipe. She turned to face him with a smile on her face, but he was frowning at his phone. Her smile faded as she returned to give Gabe and Maddy's order to the chef, keeping Green Eyes' order to herself. She waved it at the chef. "I've got this."

She cast a surreptitious glance at Green Eyes as she put together the salad, adding the leanest cuts of chicken before tossing it in the dressing. She was about to take it over when she turned and went back again. Dressing on the side! How could she forget? She repeated the exercise, before carefully pouring the dressing into one of the dinky white cream jugs. She stood back, looking with an artistic eye, before tearing off a few sprigs of coriander which was growing on the window sill, and sprinkling it artfully over the salad. There. She loved coriander.

She picked up the coffee and took them both over to the green-eyed guy.

"What's that?"

"Coriander."

"I didn't ask—"

She smiled. "You don't have to. Is there anything else?" She put her hands behind her, twisting her greenstone ring, hoping that this might be the moment. The end of the second week. Two lots of seven. It might be auspicious to someone into numbers. She had no idea. She made a mental note to check her numerology book later.

"No, nothing else, thank you."

"Right… right," she repeated, unable to think of anything that could keep her staring at the man who lingered in her mind long after he'd left the café. And at night, when she couldn't sleep in the hot small hours when she sipped her water, trying to cool her body and her mind. Water. She twisted mid step and picked up a carafe of water from the table. She turned back to him with a smile to top up his water. The smile faltered when she realized he hadn't drunk any. She topped it up anyway. A drop spilled on the table. She wiped it away with a cloth and then noticed that he'd piled all the coriander to one side.

"Don't you like coriander?" She felt strangely hurt. You didn't normally get coriander in a Caesar salad.

"No. It takes like soap."

"Soap? No, it doesn't. I wouldn't have given it to you if it did!"

His look softened slightly at her words. "It's genetic. Coriander tastes like soap to some people. And, no, I dare say you wouldn't. You don't look the type."

"Type?" Amber shifted her weight from one of her hips to the other, the personal comment making her indignation disappear. "What type do I look?"

He didn't answer for a moment and she felt the burn of his eyes on every part of her as his gaze swept over her. "You look the helpful type."

The burn lessened instantly, deflating the sensuality that his gaze had made her feel. "Helpful? I look helpful?"

"Yes." He frowned. "Is there something wrong with that?"

She felt her lips tighten and she gave the table another quick, unnecessary wipe and picked up his half-drunk coffee. "Of course not. Nothing wrong with that, I'm a waitress and waitresses should be helpful."

Then she felt his hand over hers and she drew in a sharp breath, their eyes hot on each other. "But you're also an artist."

"How do you know?"

"I saw your work in the gallery."

"How did you know it was mine?"

"It had your name on it."

"You know my name," she breathed.

He nodded to her name tag. "Yes."

"Oh. Did you like them?"

"Very much."

"Which ones did you like the best?"

"The flowers. The small ones. They're a series."

"Oh yes." She grinned. "They're all sold. The gallery owner said…" She trailed off.

"Yes, I bought them."

"All?"

"All."

"Oh." She couldn't figure out if this was flattering or vaguely creepy. She tried to pull her hand, which held the coffee cup, away from his.

"No," he said firmly. She tried to stop her hand from trembling under the enveloping strength of his touch. From the way he glanced at her hand, she doubted she'd succeeded. "I haven't finished my coffee yet," he continued.

She looked down at the half-full cup and relaxed her grip. "Of course." She walked away, confused and aroused by the touch of his hand on hers, and the look in his eyes—as if she appealed to his taste buds infinitely more than coriander. He was all contradiction: one minute slightly grumpy and critical, the other, devouring her with his eyes and revealing that he liked her art. *He liked her art*, she repeated to herself. It meant more to her than anything. Flattering, nice, and definitely *not* creepy, she decided.

She glanced back at him when she reached the counter. He was finishing his salad. When his phone beeped, he lifted it and, without answering it or even glancing at the screen, flicked it to silent and continued to eat his lunch. How did he do that? There was no way she would have been able to stop herself at least checking to see who was calling her. Such discipline. She shivered as her thoughts drifted and she tried to focus on the tasks at hand.

Maddy raised her eyebrows and nodded toward Green Eyes. Gabe looked around, wondering what was going on. Amber did a silent squee and gave a thumbs-up to Maddy, followed by an anxious look at Green Eyes, but he was looking steadily out the window at the sea.

Amber hummed to herself as she tidied the counter. Most of the lunch customers were beginning to leave—regulars, who she'd known all her life, and she chatted easily with them, catching up on the minutiae of their lives, which were as important to her as her own.

Her stomach flipped as the elderly couple she'd been talking to moved away to reveal Green Eyes, unraveling himself to his full height and walking purposefully towards her. She had to raise her head to meet his gaze. He was unsmiling as he nodded to her and withdrew his wallet.

She smiled. "I hope you enjoyed your lunch."

"I did, thank you." His green eyes seemed to caress her. She wondered if they only caressed on a full stomach because when he'd entered the café he'd looked distinctly grumpy.

He plucked out a crisp note and handed it to her. She took it between her fingers and for a brief moment they were both holding on to it. Then she tugged it and he looked momentarily surprised before he released it.

She counted out the change as she took it from the till and counted it out again as she placed it in his hands. They weren't worker's hands, no calluses that she could see, but they were large and firm and strong. She sighed and looked up into a frown.

"What? Did I get it wrong?" she asked. It was usually the case when she met a frown.

"No. Nothing wrong. Certainly nothing wrong at all. It's just... Just that I've never met anyone like you before."

She sucked in a small gasp. Not only was that *nearly* an admission that he was attracted to her, but it was also the longest sentence she'd ever heard him speak. That could only mean one thing—the moment had come. "How do you mean?"

"The way you count out the money."

"Oh," she said, her smile fading. She felt as if she were a yoyo, being swept up into a dramatic, intense grasp, only to be let fall again, plummeting to the ground. She cleared her throat. "Yes, I'm less likely to make a mistake that way.

EFTPOS is easier. No counting, you see. No mental arithmetic to trip me up."

"Ah," he said. "Well…" He sucked his teeth as if trying to work out how he could delay himself. "I'd best be going." He turned and began to walk away, which sent a blast of panic shooting through her, against which neither dignity nor self-preservation stood a chance.

She couldn't take any more U-turns. He'd bought her paintings for goodness' sake, and even *she* knew they weren't her best work. He liked her—he had to like her, there could be no other explanation for his frequent lunches at the café, for their weird conversations—and she liked him, and it appeared that if she didn't do something about it, nothing would happen.

"Would you like to have dinner with me one evening?" she shouted at his back. The café went quiet.

He came to an abrupt halt and twisted around. "What?"

She blushed as she felt all eyes on her. She wished he'd come closer so she didn't have to continue to make a fool of herself. But it seemed there was no moving him.

"Dinner," she said more loudly. "I wondered if you'd like some."

She heard a splutter from Maddy and an expletive from Gabe but refused to look their way, in case she lost her nerve.

"I've just had lunch," he said.

"I'm not talking about lunch, I'm asking you to dinner." She cleared her throat. "Tonight. At my place. Would you like to come to dinner?" Surely he understood now. She couldn't make it any plainer unless she added what she'd like to do to him after dinner. But even she had her limits to what she said in public.

"No," he said.

Her mouth fell open in shock; she felt as if she'd been

stabbed, gutted, winded. "You said 'no'?" She swayed and gripped the side of the bench for support.

"Yes, I said 'no'."

"Oh." She tried to smile but her mouth wouldn't work. She didn't understand it. Had she really misread all that body language? All those surreptitious glances? All the waves of attraction which had surged between them? "Oh," she repeated faintly, as she took a few steps back. "Why... why not?" She had to know.

"Because I don't like eating at the houses of people I don't know."

Her eyes widened. "But you... *kind* of know me..." She trailed off, realizing that he probably didn't; that all the connection could, quite possibly, be in her head.

"Amber!" Gabe called from just over her shoulder. She turned around to see Gabe looking daggers at Green-Eyes.

"Yes?"

"Dad's just called and wanted to know if you're still going to Belendroit."

"Of course I am. I told him I am."

"He wants you to call him back," Gabe insisted, glancing between the two of them.

Green Eyes was either ignoring, or oblivious to, Gabe's glare. He pocketed his wallet, nodded at Amber, and walked out the door without a backward glance.

Amber let a long, slow breath slide from her body, and looked around to find the few remaining lunch customers quickly looking back at their plates, except for Gabe, whose angry gaze was following Green Eyes out the door.

Amber walked without thinking to Maddy and slid into the seat next to her.

"Oh, Amber!" Maddy said, her beautiful face puckered into a frown.

"Bastard," muttered Gabe, taking his seat opposite Maddy.

"No, he's not," said Amber automatically. She *knew* he wasn't, or at least she *thought* she knew he wasn't.

"Yes, he is!" said an indignant Gabe. "Anyone who treats my sister like that is a total and utter bastard. And next time I see him, I'll tell him."

"No!" said Amber.

"You'll do no such thing!" Maddy added.

"Come on, he's rude and obnoxious."

Amber opened her mouth to speak but couldn't think of anything to counter Gabe's claim. "I know he comes across like that, but I see something different in him."

Gabe scoffed. "What you see is an athletic body."

"And what's wrong with that?" asked Amber.

"Nothing is wrong with that." He sighed and took her hands. "All I'm saying is that I can see him for what he is. I'm not blinded by pheromones."

"Pheromones are important," said Amber. "They are probably more truthful than words."

Gabe sighed and sat back in defeat.

"And he bought my paintings."

Gabe's eyes opened wide. "He…"

"Bought my paintings. He told me he did."

Neither Gabe nor Maddy spoke.

"Anyway." Amber chewed her lip. "It was probably the coriander."

Maddy tilted her head to one side. "Coriander?"

"Yes. He doesn't like it."

"Nor do I," said Gabe.

"Yes, you do. I always give you some."

"And I eat it because I know you think you're being generous. Anyway, what's that to do with anything?"

"I gave him some, too."

"And Green Eyes over there—" Gabe waved towards the man's retreating figure through the window. "Did he eat it?"

Amber pouted, rose and took their plates. "It doesn't matter now." She swallowed hard. "I've ruined it."

"Amber!" said Maddy and Gabe in unison, rising to follow Amber to the till.

As Gabe paid, Maddy put her arm around Amber. "You've done nothing to ruin it. Green Eyes is obviously, well, a little different to most people."

"He is, isn't he?" said Amber, her interest piqued once more. "I think that's what I first noticed." She shook her head as she glanced through the window at the retreating broad shoulders. He'd stopped for a few minutes to check his phone. "No, who am I kidding? Gabe was right." She sighed. "Just look at him."

Both Maddy and Amber watched Green Eyes flick the lights of his sleek Jaguar and open the door, without glancing around.

"He certainly looks as if he's in his own world. Sort of single-minded, focused," mused Maddy.

"Um. And when he's focused on you, it's like…"

Maddy's gaze shifted and settled on Gabe. "It's like the best thing in the world."

Amber smiled to herself to see Maddy and Gabe exchange looks. She loved love; it was that simple, particularly when it came to her family. And slowly her brothers and sisters were finding it. Lizzi, Rachel, Max and now Gabe—all married. That only left her two brothers, Rob and Cameron—neither of whom she could see settling down any time soon—and her. And her inability to spot a bastard looked like she'd end up the spinster aunt, doting on her nieces and nephews with only regrets and 'what-ifs' to fill her lonely evenings and nights.

Then she caught sight of herself in the mirror, red hair

escaping her plait in curls around her face, blue eyes bright, and she smiled at her reflection, her optimistic nature refusing to be suppressed. So what if Green Eyes had got away this time? There would be others. And she'd make sure next time that he wouldn't get away so easily. There would be no repeat of the coriander incident.

2

"*A*mber!" called Jim Connelly from the back deck of Belendroit. "Someone to see you!" It wasn't until the second call that she heard him. She rose from her cross-legged position, gave one last squint at her painting, and dabbed her paintbrush on the canvas.

"Amber!"

She tore herself from the painting of the iridescent shell, lodged in the rippling sand exposed by the receding tide, and turned to look up at the house. She waved. "Coming!"

The cocker spaniels, Stanley and Boo, jumped up and ran around, Stanley barking nervously at the sudden movement. She fondled his velvety ears, calming him, before following Boo, who was already trotting up the beach to the house.

"Someone here to see you!" repeated her father, louder, more strident this time.

She frowned. Her father sounded unusually agitated. "I'm coming!"

Who on earth could it be? No one rattled her father. Certainly none of her friends. They might infuriate him, or puzzle him, but not unnerve him. Besides, she'd be seeing them later at the pub, and it couldn't be one of the family, otherwise he wouldn't have sounded so formal.

She stomped up the steps in her charity shop Doc Martens, careful not to trip on her undone laces, and kissed Jim on the cheek. "Who is it, Pop?"

Jim shrugged, his bushy eyebrows beetling into the center. He glanced nervously over his shoulder. "I have *no* idea. He didn't say, and somehow"—he shrugged—"I didn't like to ask him."

"Really?" It wasn't like her father to be intimidated by anyone. And anyone who was likely to intimidate him was unlikely to be asking for her.

"Are you expecting anyone?" Jim asked in a tense voice that was trying to be quiet, but not succeeding.

"No." She shrugged. "Anyway, I'll just…" She began to walk into the house, but her father put a hand on her arm, stopping her abruptly.

"Shall I come with you?"

"If you think you must, but…" This was getting silly. "No, it's fine. *I'm* fine. I can look after myself."

Jim shot her a warning look full of meaning.

"Pop, I was sixteen then. I'm older now." She didn't add 'wiser' because she wasn't sure she was. She'd used to trust herself, now she rarely did.

"Well, I'll be here if you need me."

She nodded, trying to quash the nerves which were gathering in the pit of her stomach. "Okay."

"He's in the parlor."

"The parlor?" she repeated. She couldn't remember the last time they'd used the parlor. The nerves intensified, making her feel queasy. Had someone died?

"It seemed best," Jim said solemnly. "Are you okay?"

"Pop, I'll be fine." Although she was feeling less fine by the minute. Her father's hovering didn't help. "Why don't you put the kettle on? Make a pot of tea?"

She watched him walk away and only after she'd heard the rush of water into the kettle did she walk to the parlor door. She paused outside the closed door and bit her lip. This was ridiculous. It was her and her father working each other up. The rest of her family always teased them about being over-dramatic. She took a deep breath and reached out for the brass handle, dented with age, and gripped it, her grip faltering as she heard a sound behind her. Her father stood at the end of the hallway, kettle in hand, watching her. She felt strangely comforted.

She opened the door and the silhouette of a man, outlined by the bright winter sunlight, stood before the window. He was smartly dressed in a sharp suit which even Amber could see must have cost more than her monthly salary, probably her annual salary for all she knew. Then he turned and moved out of the stream of sunlight and her mouth dropped open. Those green eyes, she'd know them anywhere, even when they came along with a suit so sharp it could cut something.

"Oh, it's you!" she said, a blush blooming on her cheeks.

"Miss Connelly."

She felt as if she'd walked into a costume drama. She'd have laughed at his response if she hadn't been surprised that he knew her surname. She only ever signed her paintings with her first name, and her staff badge only had "Amber" printed on it.

Jim stood behind her, and she could sense his confusion. "Is everything all right here?" he asked protectively.

"Of course, Pop. This is a..." She couldn't say 'friend' because he was a friend only in her imagination, and she couldn't introduce him because she didn't know his name. "This is someone I met at the café."

"David Tremayne, sir," he said. "I'm sorry for the intrusion, but I wasn't sure how else to contact your daughter."

"Oh," said Jim, looking from one to the other, his confusion intensifying. And Amber could hardly question it—she was as confused as he was. Besides, she couldn't help repeating his name in her head. *David Tremayne.* It was a beautiful name, just like him. She glanced up into those green eyes, which were looking as assured as ever. They alighted on her and she took a sharp intake of breath, feeling the tingle of his gaze from her scalp to her toes.

"You weren't at the café," he said. His voice was gentler now his eyes were on her. She swallowed.

"I took a few days leave from the café to be at Belendroit while Dad recovered from an operation." There was a silence. He obviously wasn't the chatty sort. "And I've been doing some painting." Again another silence which even the usually loquacious Jim didn't fill. "Hm..." She shrugged. "And stuff like that." She frowned. Wasn't anyone else going to say anything? "So... you wanted to see me about something?"

David looked startled, as if waking up from a dream. "Yes! Sorry, I, um, wanted to apologize. For the other day."

"What for?"

"You asked me to dinner and I declined. I was wrong."

Amber ignored her father's gasp and mutterings as he stomped back into the kitchen, pulling the door closed behind him.

"You were wrong?" she repeated. "You seemed pretty certain."

"I was. I didn't want to have dinner at your place. I'm very particular about where I eat. But I *would* like to *take* you to dinner."

"Oh." She screwed up her face a moment, while she digested the fact that he had suggested that her house wasn't sanitary enough to eat in, but that he still wanted to be with her. She met those green eyes again and tried not to weaken. "Well, that's a little odd."

It was his turn to frown. "In what way?"

"In the way that you've just insulted me by saying that either my cooking, or my home, isn't good enough for you to eat in."

"It's not. I lead a very regimented life, Miss Connelly. I exercise hard, I eat carefully, and I work."

She tried not to laugh. But one glance at those stern green eyes and the laughter died. This dude wasn't joking. "Sounds very... serious."

His frown lowered, darkening those eyes. It was his turn to shrug. The movement didn't look right on him. "Of course. Why wouldn't it be?"

She laughed out loud then. And then her laughter faded as she realized he meant it. He really was being serious about being serious. "Well." She shrugged. "Sometimes people like to have fun. You must make time to have fun, surely?"

His frown didn't lift. "Miss Connelly, I'm serious about my life. I've had to be. And I'm serious about dinner."

Amber had never met anyone as intense. It did something strange to her head and her stomach. Or maybe that was simply because of the way his jacket gaped, revealing a shirt which fitted his chest snugly, and those green eyes. "Goodness!"

"So, would you care to join me for dinner on Friday at St Augustine's?"

"St Augustine's?" She thought she'd misheard. She'd only ever been there once and that had been by mistake. She certainly hadn't eaten there.

"Yes, that's right, St Augustine's. It appears to be the best restaurant around here."

She blinked twice. Was he kidding? It was the best of the best; it was so 'best' that famous people even made a detour from Christchurch to dine there. She swallowed. "Do they do vegan?"

"I've already checked. Yes, they do."

Her heart dropped. She kinda hoped they wouldn't. But her heart didn't drop too far because she was struck by the fact that (a) he knew she was vegan and (b) he'd checked.

"You knew I was vegan?"

"Yes."

"How?"

"I asked that young woman you always speak to in the café. The tall blonde who sits with the man who glares at me."

"Maddy? You asked Maddy?"

"I don't know her name."

"You didn't check *that* then?"

"No. I only wanted to find out about you."

A weird sound escaped her mouth on a sigh—something between a whimper and a laugh.

"So, would you like to come to dinner with me?"

"Well, yes, I would. Thank you. That would be nice." She smiled, and his face lit up with an earth-shattering smile which reflected her own. More than nice, she thought as she felt its effect in every single part of her body. Talk about an atomic smile. During weeks of coming to the café, he'd never smiled. But it was like the sun had burst through cloud, not only lighting up the world but making you feel glad you were alive.

He thrust his hands in his trouser pockets and rolled back on his heels, betraying his relief. She liked that.

"Good. So I'll pick you up around eight?"

"That would be lovely, thank you." It seemed Amber had become Lizzie Bennett to David's Darcy. She half-wondered if David would seek her father's permission, too.

He pressed his lips together as if to stop himself from smiling. It worked. "Good. Shall I pick you up from here?"

"Yes. I'm staying a few days more."

"Good. I'll see your father, then."

"What? Why?" He had to be kidding! But he was already out the door, striding down the hall to the kitchen where Jim Connelly was crashing around as if he were desperately trying not to hear their conversation.

"Mr. Connelly?"

David stopped suddenly and Amber nearly bumped into him. She exchanged surprised looks with her father.

"Yes?" She'd never seen her father look so alarmed with any of her, or her siblings', friends before.

David strode forward and held out his hand. "Good to meet you, sir."

Relieved that he wasn't about to have some unwelcome revelation foisted on him, Jim gripped his hand in a very firm handshake. "And you, David." It seemed her father had come to the same decision about his name as she did. "And call me Jim."

"Will do, Jim. I'll see you on Friday, then."

The alarmed look returned to Jim's face. "Friday?" he repeated faintly.

Amber took pity on him. "David is going to pick me up. We're going to dinner at St Augustine's on Friday."

"St Augustine's?" Jim looked from one to the other.

"That's right, sir." David corrected himself. "Jim. I'll come by at eight."

He turned to Amber. "Goodbye, Amber. And thank you for agreeing to come."

Her heart nearly stopped when he said her name. The second syllable came out like a little puff, causing his beautiful lips to pout slightly. She cleared her throat. "My pleasure." She was sure it would be.

His lips curved into another of his rare smiles and she lifted her eyes to his. The smile lingered in the green of his eyes long after his lips resumed their usual stern shape.

David glanced at Jim and nodded before turning and descending the steps with a purposeful tread. She liked how sure he always was—so opposite to herself. She sighed as he got into his dark blue Jaguar and drove carefully across the potholed drive. Amber winced as the car bounced and crunched over a rutted area which had suffered at the hands of her habit of parking on boggy ground, now dried hard, and an errant tree root. The car disappeared among the trees which lay between the house and the road. She waited as she heard him pull out smoothly onto the highway and drive off towards Akaroa.

She shook her head in disbelief. Green-Eyes, David, here to see her. She twisted her mouth into a grin. He must like her. She called for the dogs who'd trotted after the car and sat staring at where it had disappeared into the trees as if they, too, couldn't quite believe what had just happened.

She walked back to her father, who still held a kettle in his hands. She took it from him with a grin and went inside the house. After a moment Jim and the dogs followed.

"Did he…"

"Did he what, Dad?"

"Did he just call me Sir Jim?"

Amber burst out laughing and continued to laugh as she placed the kettle on the kitchen bench. "I think he did, although I don't think he meant to."

Jim grunted. "I doubt there are many things that young man does without meaning to. He's, well… He's quite unlike any of your other young men, Amber."

Amber flicked the switch on the kettle and turned to face her father. "That, my dear father, can only be a good thing."

"Yes, indeed." Jim replied, but Amber noticed he didn't

look convinced. But he would be, or at least she hoped he would be, because Amber had never been as attracted, or as intrigued, by a man in all her life.

∾

AMBER RAN out of the sea toward Flo's Backpacker's Lodge.

She grabbed her towel and bag and opened the small gate that stood between Flo's back veranda and the beach. The main living room was already crowded with people. She shouldn't have stopped for a swim, but she couldn't help herself. Deferring her gratification wasn't her strong suit.

"Sorry I'm late," Amber mouthed to Flo as she sat cross-legged on the floor. The others shifted along for her. Flo smiled and looked up at the long-haired, earnest man standing up. He swallowed and began talking.

"Thanks to Flo for letting us use her place. But we all know why we're here."

"Too right!" someone called out. "They can't keep on getting away with it!"

"Precisely. Sterling Property Holdings are true to form and continue to ignore our protests about demolishing historic houses in central Christchurch."

"They called Tiritea a slum!" said Flo.

"It's not a slum," said Amber, looking indignantly from Flo to the speaker. "It's beautiful."

"It *is* beautiful," affirmed the young man, smiling at Amber. "*And* it's important. It's the birthplace of one of our foremost citizens—someone who we have to thank for all the past work on saving our beautiful land—and is a prime example of early colonial architecture."

"And EarthFoods wouldn't find anywhere else as cheap to operate from."

There were mutterings of agreement to this. EarthFoods

was an organic health foods cooperative with little money to spend on fighting the huge conglomerates that wanted to develop the old, neglected quarter of Christchurch. Earth-Foods' major shareholder was Amber, who'd used the inheritance she'd received from her mother to keep the company afloat.

"So what can we do?" asked Amber.

"Ah," the man said eagerly, leaning forward toward Amber. "That's where you come in."

"Me? What can I do? I don't have any more money, I'm afraid. You want me to bake?"

"No, I want you to create your art."

Amber blinked and shook her head in confusion. "I don't see how my little paintings can help."

"That's because they're little. What I'm suggesting is something much, much bigger." He looked around at the small group. "What we need is more of Amber's rainbows except on a larger scale. It's Amber's rainbows which have drawn the little attention we've garnered. And we need to double down on that."

Amber jumped up as a vision of what she could do filled her head. "I could do one large rainbow on the side of the building, with birds over it, and fish under it and hills, rolling out behind it all."

The man sat back in his chair with a big grin. "Exactly. A vision of nature which fits with conservation and fits with EarthFoods' ethos. And, more to the point, a vision which will catch the public's attention. Perhaps then we'll get enough support to stop the destruction of Christchurch's heritage buildings."

He sat back as people cheered and clapped. Someone popped open a bottle of elderflower champagne and poured it into the tumblers which Flo had brought out. Flo was listening as the original speaker expounded on the importance of their mission. She rolled her eyes at Amber who nodded towards the door. Flo excused herself and joined Amber outside in the rear garden which fronted onto the road.

"I can't wait to get started on those rainbows!"

"It's illegal though, Amber. I mean, you guys have a water-tight lease on the building. But that doesn't cover painting."

"It'll be fine. No one's ever gone to prison for painting a rainbow," said Amber, peering around the corner of the house.

"You've got a point there. And, besides, it'll create the kind of publicity which they don't want."

"Ha! Peaceful protest at its most effective. Sterling Properties is scared we're going to win over public opinion. And we can't fail to with rainbows! No one can resist a rainbow."

Flo grimaced. "Don't count on it."

Amber jumped up and stood in the only place in the garden where the road and pavement could be seen. She turned to smile at Flo, who looked at her suspiciously.

"Why are you so fidgety?"

"No reason," Amber said, pushing open the gate and looking up and down the street. She relaxed. There was no sign of him, so she hadn't missed him. He ran this stretch of road like clockwork.

"Are you waiting for someone?"

Amber blushed and shrugged. "Not exactly waiting..." More like hoping, she thought to herself. "Anyway, I wanted to know what your reaction was to the news."

"What news?"

Amber's heart sank. She'd known Gabe and Maddy were having dinner with Flo last week, and so had told Gabe to tell her. He must have chickened out.

Amber licked her bottom lip uncertainly. She raised her eyebrows and grimaced a little. "About Rob?"

Her delicate approach didn't appear to do anything to ease the blow. Amber could see it in Flo's face—the pain was heartfelt. Amber reached out to Flo. "Oh, Flo, I'm so sorry."

Flo flung open her hands. "Nothing to be sorry about. I…" She trailed off. The defensive expression fell and she jumped up, turning her back on Amber in a way which Amber recognized. It was what Flo did when she wanted to hide her feelings. But Amber wasn't one to let someone grieve on their own.

She put her arm around Flo, pressing her head to hers. "It was a long time ago. I'm sure things will be fine."

Flo twisted her face away from Amber. "Fine. Absolutely *fine*." She placed the emphasis on the last word.

"I know it's not what you wanted. Fine is nothing compared to what you two had."

Flo breathed in deeply. "Fine is all I want, believe me, Amber. Your big brother and me are over, long gone, dead as a moa. It was just a bit of a shock, that's all. I didn't think he'd return. Thought his big life in London would keep him there forever."

"Really?"

"Yes, really. He can have all the beautiful girls he likes there."

Amber felt the bitterness in Flo's words as if they were a knife to her own heart. Her eyes smarted. "He was young and stupid, Flo. And I'm sure he regrets what he did with all his heart."

"His heart?" scoffed Flo. "That's a good one." Then she huffed at the sight of Amber's tears. "Look, I'm sorry. I know he's your big brother but he was a bastard to me and I can't say I've waited with bated breath for him to return to Akaroa." She sighed, and dead-headed a rose with unnecessary force. "Still, I guess I can lie low for a few weeks until he returns to the big smoke."

"Oh, no! He's not coming for a holiday, Flo. He's here to stay; he's back for good."

This was obviously too much for Flo. She walked to the end of the garden by the road and Amber's gaze followed. Just then she saw what she'd been keeping a watchful eye for. A head—a very handsome head with short cropped hair and a strong profile—bobbing up over the top of the high fence at regular intervals. Amber ran up to the front gate just as the bobbing head reached it.

"Hi!" she called out.

David stopped abruptly. "Amber. What are you doing here?"

She laughed. "Visiting a friend. It's not so unusual. I do live near here."

He followed her glance toward her house and nodded. "It's just that you're usually at the café."

"Afternoon off." She breathed deeply of him—a beautifully clean, outdoorsy sweaty smell which made her mouth water. It nearly made her lose focus, nearly made her forget what she'd wanted to say. But as he jiggled on his feet as if to run away, she focused. "I was about to go to the beach. Do you want to come?"

His gaze remained on her face. She pulled the towel from around her neck, leaving her upper half clad only in the brief, damp bikini. It was revealing, but then she often went skinny dipping at Belendroit, much to her family's irritation. They didn't seem to understand how joyous it was to feel the cool water and moonlight on your skin, as if you were a part of nature.

But still his gaze didn't falter. Her heart plummeted. Didn't he like her?

"No, I have other things to do." His expression didn't change. She had no idea what he was thinking. He stepped back a few paces and it was all she could do not to jump the

31

gate, and him. "But I'll pick you up on Friday at eight. Right?"

"Right," she said, echoing his business-like manner. "Definitely right."

"Right," he repeated. "See you then."

She walked out the gate and watched him run off without a backward glance. She turned to see Flo leaning on the fence watching them, her good humor returned.

"What was that all about?"

Amber sighed and shook her head. "I don't know. He's hot, right? And he's asked me out. But that's not like until the weekend—"

"And waiting isn't your strong suit."

"Exactly. So I thought"—she shrugged and plucked at her bikini top—"that he might like to join me at the beach.

"Ah, so you thought you'd lure him with your womanly curves to the beach for some tumbling in the sand."

"You know me so well," Amber replied with a smile. "But he's not interested." She watched as David turned up a nearby street. "Hang on a minute! Where's he going?" She squinted into the light as she watched David let himself into a front door with a key. She pointed to him and turned to Flo. "Does he live there?" She looked back as the door closed on him. "I didn't know he lived there! Flo! What do you know?"

"Not a lot. I know that the old cottage was knocked down and that new modern house was built in its place. And I also know that you've got it right—that man is definitely hot. Scorching in fact."

"Maybe he lives there."

"No. I'd have noticed. Believe me."

Amber felt her heart twist into a soggy knot. "Scorching maybe, but he doesn't seem to be scorching for me. He hardly looks at me."

"He must like you, otherwise he wouldn't have asked you out."

"I guess," she said doubtfully.

"You really like this guy?"

"Yes, I really like this guy. He's gorgeous and cute and funny. Although, to be honest, I'm not so sure he means to be funny, but he is. He's a darling."

Flo snorted. "'Darling' isn't the word I'd have used to describe him, but then, hey, what do I know? I stuffed up the only meaningful relationship I've ever had."

Amber glanced at her friend, whose face had dropped once more. "You didn't stuff it up, my stupid brother did."

She flung her arm around Flo and they walked back through the beautiful gardens on which Flo lavished all the energy and love that she'd once reserved for Amber's brother, Rob.

"What you need to do, Amber, is to wow this guy when you go out so that he has no chance of walking away."

"Wow him? Hm, I'm not sure I can do that."

"Where is it you're going to dinner?"

"St Augustine's."

"Oh! That's not your usual stamping ground."

"I know. I've no idea what to wear. But Rachel will. She's been there loads."

"Oh, Amber! You're not Rachel! Wear your usual clothes; don't try to be someone you're not!"

"But that someone is what gorgeous David wants!"

"Well, let him find that someone elsewhere."

Amber shrugged. "It's just 'dressing up' like we used to do when we were kids. And it just might make him see me in a different way."

"Honey." Flo stopped outside the open French windows and took hold of Amber's hands. "You're you, and you'll always be you, so why pretend to be anyone different?"

Before Amber could answer, Flo was called back into the house and Amber was left alone. Her gaze drifted back in the general direction of where she'd seen David disappear into a house in which she was sure he didn't live. Where had he gone? Why all the mystery? And why did he ask her out if he wasn't attracted to her? She sighed. Flo was wrong. Nothing wrong with a bit of dress up.

*a*mber had spent the afternoon on the phone spreading the news that Green Eyes—she really would have to try to stop herself from calling him that—had asked her out, and trying to find a dress which would allow her to fit into St Augustine's. Flo had told her not to worry, that she should be true to herself and wear the orange floaty number with the purple fringe. But she'd managed to contact her big sister Rachel overseas and she'd come to the rescue by offering one of her dresses, obviously under the misapprehension that Amber was leaving behind her hippy phase. Amber didn't have the heart to correct her beautiful sister.

The remaining hours before David came to pick her up were spent altering said dress to make it fit. Rachel was curvier than Amber but Rachel had given Amber permission to do whatever she wanted with it. So Amber attacked it with her mother's pinking shears and the sewing machine.

"And I don't know why he's waiting until eight to pick you up. A bit late, if you ask me," said Jim, flicking on the outside lights and peering through the curtains of the unlit drawing room.

"Pop! What are you doing?"

"Being prepared," he murmured. "Like a good boy scout."

"You're a bit old to be a boy scout," she mumbled as she adjusted the straps of her dress and smoothed the wrinkled seam across her hips. It wasn't haute couture but it was the only thing she had suitable for St Augustine's. Not that she'd ever been there, but Rachel had told her what to expect —*glamor*. She caught her anxious expression in the mirror. She didn't do glamor, but she'd give it a go. For tonight, at least.

"Amber!" called Jim from the hall where he stood in darkness. "He's coming. I'm sure I heard his car."

Amber padded down the hall in her bare feet, flicked on the light and went into the drawing room. She sat on the couch and pulled on her shoes. "Don't sound so alarmed, Pop."

"I just want you to be ready." He came into the room and his face fell. "You're not even ready yet!"

"I am *nearly*. What's the panic, anyway?"

Jim pointed in the direction of the car whose lights briefly tracked around the uncurtained room. "That man… he'll be here any minute and he'll expect you to be ready."

She stood up, gingerly testing her walk in the high heels which Rachel had insisted she wear, and did a double-take when she caught sight of herself in the mirror. She hardly recognized herself. She frowned, plucked a tissue from a nearby box, and blotted her lips. She sighed at her reflection —too late now to do anything about it—and glanced at her father in the reflection. "That man has a name. David."

"Whatever, he's coming, and you're not ready."

"Well, lucky for me that I'm not as scared of him as you appear to be."

"Scared? I'm not…" Jim jumped as a car door slammed, ringing out like a gunshot in the crisp evening air. He met

Amber's glance in the mirror. "Okay, you got me. That man of yours is the scariest bloke I've ever met. I thought your big brother Max was macho enough, but this one"—he blew out his cheeks—"sure takes the cake. He's terrifying. He's the sort you see in films who'll step in front of a gun and kill his enemy before they can draw breath."

"Pop! Don't be silly. The only thing David kills are business deals… He's into finance, accounting or property or something." She frowned. "Something like that." She sprayed on a little perfume.

"Well, he's certainly not like your usual type."

"What do you mean? I don't have a type." She did, but she wasn't in the mood to agree.

"Yes, you do. Dreamy chaps, usually with no jobs, and a penchant for poetry. Dudes, beach bums, call them what you will."

Amber cocked her head in the mirror just as there was a knock on the door. She turned and smiled brightly at her father, who'd instinctively backed away from the door. "Well, this *dude* is a serious dude. I'd have thought you'd have liked that."

"I'd like it if you went to the door."

"Okay, okay." She picked up her antique evening bag, its sequins showering multi-colored light across the room, and gave her dad a kiss, smudging her cherry red lipstick from his cheek with her thumb. "Don't wait up."

"I most certainly *will*. You be careful, young lady."

"Don't worry, I'll check to make sure he hasn't got a gun." She shook her head at his suddenly alarmed expression. "*Pop*… I'm joking!"

Her high heels clicked on the wooden floor as she approached the door. The outside light revealed David's tall outline, and a gorgeous sensation of nerves and attraction skittered and fluttered in her belly. Not the kind of nerves her father had, but something far more earthy. As she opened the door and she met those intense eyes boring straight into her, speaking directly to her soul, the fizzing turned to an effervescent buzz which reassured her that the only danger she was in from this man was some damned good loving.

"Good evening," she said brightly, using the formality that David seemed to expect.

"Amber," he breathed, as she stepped out under the bright light. "You look beautiful."

She did a mental fist punch. The dress had worked! She'd expected a formal good evening, maybe an arm extended to aid her across the uneven lawn to the car. Instead she received a caress with his eyes and a lowered voice which wound its way sensuously inside her and tugged a little somewhere where it probably shouldn't have, not with her dad watching, anyway. She glanced over her shoulder. Jim cleared his throat and stomped up the hall to them, holding onto the door handle for dear life. "Enjoy your evening." He nodded uncomfortably. "Must be off now." He flashed a brief, uncertain grin at David. "Things to do."

"See you later, Pop!"

"Good night, sir… Jim." David quickly corrected himself.

Jim frowned and shook his head before closing the door on them.

She shivered under David's gaze and her silky wrap slithered from her shoulders and pooled onto the worn wood of the veranda. He picked it up and placed around her, his fingertips brushing her bare shoulders. She shivered again, and it had nothing to do with the soft rain which had begun to fall.

"Are you cold?"

"No."

He nodded slowly. "Good."

Amber had never felt so self-conscious in her life as they

walked down the steps, she hurrying a little to keep up with his long stride. He opened the car door for her and she slid onto the leather seat. He closed the door and she inhaled again—leather, and some kind of expensive aftershave, the like of which she'd never come across before. She'd have to describe it to Rachel to identify it. Whatever it was, it made her mouth water. He got into the seat beside her and switched on the ignition. The motor purred into life and they bounced their way carefully across the drive.

"Your father's drive could do with leveling. I'll get someone onto it on Monday."

"No," she said, alarmed at the thought of how her dad would react. "No, thank you, but no. Pop wouldn't want you to go to any bother for him."

"It's no bother. I'll have someone call him Monday morning and arrange a time."

She shrugged. She'd let Pop sort that one out.

They pulled out from the bumpy drive onto the empty coast road and headed towards Akaroa, nestled darkly under the lowering cloud. Despite how fast David drove, he didn't drive recklessly, but with the same intense concentration and focus he appeared to apply to everything in his life.

"Tell me about yourself, Amber."

"Sure. What would you like to know?"

"Everything." He glanced at her with a warm smile and she gave a small inward sigh as she melted a little more. Their gazes tangled, and she looked away as the warmth rose and suffused her face. She fixed her gaze out the window, not sure if she could trust herself not to undo the seat belt and reach up and press her lips to his. She grinned as she realized she wasn't sure which would surprise him most—the undoing of the seatbelt or the kiss.

"*Everything* is a lot to cram into a short drive."

"Okay, begin with things you like."

39

She smiled to herself as she remembered the rainbow which had emerged from the misty rain clouds over the harbor earlier that day. "I like rainbows very much."

"Rainbows?"

"Yes, rainbows. You know, those things which stretch across the sky in colors which seem too impossible for nature."

"Yes, I know what a rainbow is. A spectrum of light caused by dispersion of light in water droplets. And, actually, the colors are entirely possible in nature."

She turned to him and saw a ghost of a smile on his lips. "You're having me on! No one could look at a rainbow and think of science."

"I didn't say I thought of science. Just that it has a scientific explanation. Anyway, I can imagine you and rainbows," he said, as they slowed behind a small car. He checked the rearview mirror.

"Don't you like them?" she asked.

He shrugged as he changed gear and overtook the car. He didn't reply until he had returned to the correct side of the road and was speeding along a stretch of straight road. "They're okay. Actually, they're pretty much the bane of my life at the moment."

"How can rainbows be troublesome?"

"They appear where they shouldn't. Anyway, I don't want to talk shop. I'd much rather hear about you. Tell me about what's important to you."

"Ah, that's easy. Family. I have a heap of brothers and sisters. You've met Gabe, one of my brothers."

"The one who shoots me dirty looks?"

"That's the one."

"Ah, well, now I see why. He's protecting you. That's good. I like that."

"Do you?" It seemed a curious thing to say.

"Yes. A brother should look out for his sister."

"Yes, well, I have four brothers looking out for me. Well, strictly speaking, only two, as two of them are overseas. Max lives in Queenstown and seems to think it's also his role in life to keep an eye on me. Honestly, you'd think I'm twelve, not twenty-one."

She glanced across to find him studying her before he looked back at the road. "They love you and want to make sure you're safe. It's as simple as that."

His voice had gentled and he cleared his throat as if trying to rid the emotion which had crept into him.

"It sounds as if you have a sister you care for."

His eyes narrowed slightly and the muscles around his mouth tightened. "Yes."

"Ah-ha! I thought so. I bet you make her life a nightmare." She grinned but he didn't.

"I hope not. Tell me about your sisters."

She looked straight ahead at the road which twisted and turned its way around the harbor toward the exclusive restaurant, wondering why he didn't elaborate.

"Lizzi is the eldest, and then Rachel. Both now very happily married with children. You'll probably see Rachel if you hang around Akaroa. She and her husband and children are due back from the US next week. She's a TV star, you know."

"Oh."

"You don't find that fascinating?"

"What?"

"The fact that she's on TV—she's a TV chef. Most people are intrigued. But you're not?"

"Not particularly. Although, if she's anything like you, I'm sure I'll like her."

"You like me?"

All the tension from his mouth had gone now and he

41

smiled and shifted his warm gaze onto her. "Yes, I like you, Amber. Otherwise I wouldn't be taking you out to dinner."

"Good. Because, you know, I quite like you, too."

"Yes, I'm aware of that." The warm feeling left her.

"How?"

He flicked the car's indicator and they turned into the entrance of the restaurant. He waited until he'd drawn up directly outside the grand portico entrance before switching off the engine and looking at her.

"Because you flirt outrageously with me every time I see you, and I've noticed you don't do it with other people. Besides, I don't think you'd be able to hide your feelings from anyone."

She narrowed her eyes. "What am I feeling now?"

"You're irritated because I can read you like a book."

She shot him a look of mock indignation. "You can only read what I allow you to read."

"All I can say is that I like what you allow me to read." He ducked his head to look at the doorman who was walking over to them. He jumped out of the car and came around to her side and opened the door for her. She couldn't ever remember anyone doing that for her.

David tossed the car keys to the doorman who slid into the car and drove it away to park.

"I've only ever seen that done in films before," she said, slipping her hand through his arm as they entered the restaurant.

"Really?" he said, with the surprise of someone who was accustomed to people doing things for him. He shrugged. "It's just easier."

"Good evening, Mr. Tremayne," said the maître d', who appeared from nowhere, all ingratiating smile and subservient body language. It made Amber uneasy. She had an urge to tell him to stop it. "Good to see you again."

"And you, Paul. This is Amber Connelly."

"Miss Connelly. Pleased to meet you. Are you a relative of Rachel Connelly?"

"Yes, she's my sister."

"Ah." He beamed broadly. "A very talented and beautiful lady. Please"—he stepped to one side and swept his arm in a flourish—"follow me."

They followed him through the restaurant to a more secluded corner which overlooked the harbor and the distant lights of Akaroa. The maître d' pulled out a chair for Amber and continued to talk to David as Amber gazed out the window. From Akaroa, she'd often looked up at the twinkling restaurant lights high in the hills, but had never been tempted to go. It wasn't her kind of place. But she was here now. She glanced across the table at David, who was frowning at the wine list. She suspected he did everything with extreme care and thoroughness. A shiver ran through her body as her imagination strayed.

"Do you have a preference?" David asked.

For a moment she couldn't think what he was referring to.

"Wine. Any type of wine you prefer?"

"Yes, I mean no. I don't often drink," she added. "I mean I drink, preferably something that sparkles, but not alcohol, not when I'm out, anyway. Water, actually. Mostly water." She was babbling. She knew she was, but she felt she might be disappointing this urbane, sophisticated and totally hot man by this admission.

"Oh." He closed the wine list decisively. For a moment she wondered if he was put off by her admission, that he'd suddenly realized what a hick hippy chick he'd landed himself with, but then he looked up at her and gave her that rare smile which melted her from the inside out. It wasn't that it was a broad grin which revealed perfect teeth—

43

although it was—it was that it was like a spark which lit up his whole face. "Then nor shall I." She sighed under the delicious beam of his smile and he turned to the maître d'. "A bottle of your best sparkling water please."

In an effort to quell the blush which had been summoned by his smile, she looked around, trying to take her mind off his hair. It was cut short, tamed to within an inch of its life, and drew attention to his bone structure—classically proportioned, she thought with her artist's eye, and strong. He had the kind of head sculptors made studies of.

"See anyone you know?" he asked.

She swung back to face him and shook her head. Not least because her mind had been filled with the beauty of his head, not the other diners. She looked around once more, taking in the expensive but minimalist decor and the expensive but *not* minimalist clientele. The women's ears and necks glittered with exquisite jewelry, the men's dark suits providing a perfect foil to the glamor of the women.

"Nope. Not a soul. It's weird. I'm not used to being with strangers. Wherever I go I usually know someone. To be honest, I always make sure wherever I go I have people I know with me."

"Really? Why is that?"

She'd said too much, as usual. She didn't want to go there —not yet, anyway. She gave an ambiguous shrug. "Oh, you know... Anyway, what about you? Know anyone here?"

He didn't shift his gaze. "Not that I've noticed. I prefer to go where I don't know people."

"That's probably because you haven't lived long in one place."

"No, it's more to do with the fact that I'm not keen on people."

She opened her eyes wide. "You're not keen on people?" She shook her head in disbelief. "What does that mean?"

One side of his mouth hitched up in a brief grin. "I prefer my own company. Usually," he added, in response to her expression. "But, obviously, I want to be with you tonight. Now. Just the two of us." He looked up in relief as the maître d' brought over the sparkling water and poured them both a glass. Amber couldn't help be flattered that David sounded a little nervous, too.

She smiled her thanks at the maître d', who silently vanished into the shadows, leaving them in an intimate space —just themselves and the shadowy view of the purple-hazed hills and jewel-like lights sprinkled over them.

"So how come you've managed to avoid people?"

His brow furrowed in a delicious uncertainty which made him look boyish. "I'm with people all the time, but I do what I have to do and then move on."

"Wow, that sounds kind of clinical."

He shrugged. "I suppose it is. But I don't wish to have a relationship with every person I see. That would be ludicrous."

"Then I guess I'm ludicrous, because that's exactly what I want."

"You're not ludicrous in the least. Not in the *least*," he repeated.

She narrowed her eyes in playful challenge. "Are you repeating that to try to convince yourself?"

"No. We're different people, you and I, Amber, and I like you all the more because of it."

She sat back in her chair in surprise. "Oh! That's lovely. And unusual. Most people don't like what they don't understand."

"I didn't say I didn't understand you, because I think I do. I'm just not like you."

"So I'm easy to understand, am I?"

"Yes."

"Well, so are you. I bet I can guess what you're thinking now."

"And what's that?"

She surveyed his face. His eyes warmed with interest as he sat back and surveyed her right back. He wore a tie but his tanned neck was strong and was asking to be kissed. Goodness, she wanted to leap right across the table and taste his neck. She knew what he'd smell like—all male and clean and delicious. She swallowed and his eyes darkened and narrowed slightly.

She cleared her throat and smiled up at the waiter who topped up her glass. "Same as me, I do believe."

"Then"—he nodded to the waiter—"I think we're both in for a good night."

"I'll drink to that," she said, feeling dangerously flirtatious. The glasses clinked as the waiters appeared laden with dishes. "But I haven't ordered."

"I've already ordered. I spoke to the chef last night and gave him instructions to offer the best vegan menu he could create. I hope you don't mind?"

She should mind, but she found herself shaking her head. She was always in control of every aspect of her life but now, with those green eyes—which she could now see were shot with threads of gray and amber—fixing her with their direct gaze, she suddenly found she didn't mind in the least.

DAVID TREMAYNE SAT BACK in his chair, feeling more relaxed than he'd felt in a long time. He couldn't take his eyes off Amber—her red hair had worked its way out of the comb, which had held it loosely when he'd first picked her up. It framed her face like a halo of orange, making her blue eyes brighter. They always sparkled—it was the first thing he noticed about her—but now they positively glowed. And her lips—the way the crimson lipstick smeared a little from being over-enthusiastic with a napkin. It was all he could do to stop himself from leaning over and wiping it away with his finger, or, even better, his lips. He topped up her sparkling water.

This wasn't going at all in the way he'd intended. Get to know the enemy—seduce them, or her, if necessary—and then eliminate the opposition. No adverse publicity, only a woman to let down gently after it was all done and dusted. That had been his reason for checking her out at the café, and for asking her out. He had to admit that, after that first time when he'd seen her in the street, and he'd felt a bolt of lightning attraction between them, it hadn't been hard for him to carry out his plan. After all, it would be the best, least headline-grabbing, way of securing the future of his new project. But he hadn't banked on this at all.

He forced himself to concentrate on what she was saying. It wasn't that he didn't enjoy listening to her. She made him laugh, which was more than could be said of most people. And her worldview was so different to his as to be refreshing. Being with Amber made him forget about things, made him more optimistic about the future. That people could live in the world and be so innocent of bad things awoke in him something he thought had died—his own innocence.

But now, as the evening had progressed, listening to her had taken a back seat to admiring her. His attraction to her had been instant, some kind of physical magnetism which he'd heard about but would never have believed existed if he hadn't experienced it himself.

Then, when he'd seen her earlier in the week on the bench seat overlooking the sea between two people with disabilities, chatting away, making them laugh while, at the same time, helping them eat the chocolate brownies she'd brought out to them from the café, he'd felt something clunk inside of him. Literally. Like something falling into place. And it hadn't moved since. But it had become a part of him wherever he went. Even in meetings he'd be aware of a part of Amber in his thoughts, he'd wonder what she was doing, what her views would be of the people who were presenting to him. She was like a virus... but in a good way. But it wouldn't last and then his life would be back to normal. Except better, because he'd have quietly eliminated all opposition to his new business venture.

He sighed quietly to himself as he drank in her eyes, her oval face and her finely drawn lips which, he noticed in surprise, weren't moving. He looked up, alarmed, into her eyes once more. One fair eyebrow was raised and laughter sparkled in her eyes.

"Have you been listening to a thing I've been saying, Mr. Tremayne?"

Before he could answer he felt a warm possessive hand clamp on his shoulder. He turned to see an ex girlfriend— one from whom he'd had difficulty extricating himself— glaring at Amber.

"David!" she said, turning that cool gaze on him. "What a surprise. Haven't seen you around in a while."

He rose and kissed her proffered cheek. "Katherine," he said. "I didn't expect to see you here."

"Obviously." Her gaze returned to Amber.

"Katherine, I'd like to introduce you to Amber. Amber, this is Katherine Jones, an old friend."

Katherine raised one delicately plucked eyebrow at the epithet and extended her hand to Amber. "How lovely to meet David's latest."

David winced at the inference. As if Amber was one of a long line; she was nothing like any that had come before, and there had been a lot of them.

Amber rose and shook hands with Katherine. "Nice to meet you, Katherine."

David couldn't help but compare Katherine's lush curves clad in a figure-hugging black dress to the light that was Amber. Even their voices reinforced the difference. Katherine's mid-Atlantic accent had a studied, sultry tone while Amber's was true Kiwi and clear as a bell. He liked that. There was no pretense with Amber. He looked back at Katherine, who forced a smile as she looked from Amber to David. She let Amber's hand slip as if sensing an opposing force, and one stronger than her own.

"Anyway," Katherine fixed her smile on her face. "I'll leave you to your little tête-à-tête." She turned and inclined herself to him, revealing a cleavage which he had to admit was impressive. "See you around, David." She kissed her finger and placed it on his lips in an embarrassing display of intimacy.

She walked away, and he turned back to Amber in time to see her eyes widen in confusion.

"Everything all right, Amber?"

Her mouth twitched as if trying to summon a smile which refused to surface. "Why wouldn't it be?"

"Because you've been silent for the first time all night."

"Oh, yes, that." She shrugged and sighed and pushed her food to the side of her plate.

"Isn't the food to your liking? I'll have them bring something else." He raised his hand to attract the waiter.

"No, the food's wonderful. But I seem to have lost my appetite."

The waiter came over and cleared away the plates. David frowned and folded his arms on the table. "What's the matter? Is it something I've said?"

"No."

"Do you feel okay?"

"I did until Katherine came over."

"Ah." He sat back. "I see."

Amber folded arms on the table. "I'm not sure you do."

"You're wondering about her and me. Whether there's anything going on between us?"

"No. I could see that there wasn't. I might come across a bit scatty, but I'm not stupid, David."

"I didn't for one moment think you were. Otherwise, I can assure you, I wouldn't be here with you."

His remark appeared to annoy her even more. "Oh, so you usually check a girl's IQ before you date her?"

"I don't need to. I can tell if she's intelligent enough for me."

"I'm surprised anyone is."

"Frankly, so am I." Her comments were beginning to rankle. She shot him an annoyed glance. "I'm sorry, I'm being a jerk. We seem to be going off track here. She's simply a woman I once dated. It's not something which should put you off your dinner."

"If you want to know what put me off my dinner, it was the way she flashed her breasts at you."

"Her breasts?" he repeated, buying time.

"Yes. And don't tell me you didn't notice."

"Well, of course I did. She makes sure everyone notices."

"And you date people like that?"

"Yes, I can say that I've exclusively dated people with breasts."

"Oh," huffed Amber. "This is getting silly. You know that's not what I mean. I think I should leave now."

Panic filled him. He hadn't secured her interest, let alone her support. "No! I mean, please don't leave yet, Amber. I'm sorry, I didn't mean to be flippant but the truth is that Katherine isn't worth discussing. I'm here with you, not her, because I *want* to be with *you*, not her."

"Then I feel sorry for her because I don't think it's over for her."

And Amber looked so sorrowful that David almost felt guilty about not loving Katherine.

"I don't think Katherine would like that, and I don't think she needs that. I think Katherine will be absolutely fine. In fact she already appears to have a new beau." A very wealthy one if the cut of Katherine's partner's dinner jacket was anything to go by.

Amber's eyebrows narrowed as she leaned across the table. "David, you can tell me to mind my own business, but there's something I'd really like to know."

"Ask away."

"Did you ever love her?"

David grunted in amusement at Amber's direct question. So many women would have prevaricated, created a situation when none existed but not his Amber. He was shocked for a moment at the possessive way his thoughts were going. Then he acknowledged it and realized he was fine with it.

"No."

"No? That's it?"

"Yes, that's it. I didn't love her."

"But how long did it go on for and when did it finish?"

"We were together for about a year, I think. And it finished about six months ago."

"Oh, so recently then. That would explain her attitude."

"Attitude?"

"Yes. As if I was encroaching on her territory."

"I'm not territory."

"I think you are, to her, anyway."

"I can assure you it's over. Our relationship was…" He hesitated. "Of a certain kind." He didn't want to bring up the subject of sex with Amber. Somehow it seemed too dirty to discuss with her the foundation upon which his relationship with Katherine had been based.

"You mean it was about sex."

"Sex," he repeated, surprised again.

"Yes. You know when two people make love."

He leaned in to Amber, not wanting anyone to overhear his part in the conversation at least. From the faces that had suddenly turned in their direction, he suspected that other diners were hearing Amber's crystal clear voice, which never wavered, never changed according to its audience. "There was little 'making love' about it."

"Just sex then."

He glanced around at the amused glance of a nearby couple. "Amber!" He ran his finger around his collar which was feeling increasingly tight. "Could you keep your voice down?"

"Why? Sex is nothing to be ashamed of."

He opened his mouth but could find nothing to say. She continued to surprise him.

"I didn't say I was ashamed of anything, it's just that I prefer to keep some things private. Anyway," he said, desperately trying to think of something to change the subject, "let's talk about something else."

Amber glanced over to where Katherine was sitting, the picture of sexy sophistication. He wondered what he'd ever seen in Katherine. His eyes slipped to her figure and he suddenly remembered. But it hadn't been enough.

Amber sighed and tugged at her dress, the seams of which appeared strangely puckered. He made a mental note to introduce her to a Christchurch designer where the clothes would be made to fit her petite figure.

"What would you like to talk about?" she asked.

"You." He replied without thinking because it was the

absolute truth. "You," he repeated with emphasis. "Tell me about your family."

His honesty was rewarded by a sweet smile which lit her face up once more. "Ah, love 'em, love 'em, love 'em."

He frowned. "What, all of them?"

"Yes! My dad, all four brothers, two sisters, and nieces and nephews. Of course they're all different, all weird in some ways, but wonderful ways. Weird or strange, I love them all."

He raised his eyebrows and then lowered them in consternation. "That's a lot of love."

She looked puzzled. "Love isn't finite; it's not a limited thing. There's plenty to go around."

He surprised himself by instinctively hoping that some might be coming his way. "So tell me about them."

"I'll do better than that. Why don't you come around at the weekend when everyone will be there and I can introduce you?"

Alarm bells rang. He really could do without an audience to his seduction of the enemy. But then Katherine laughed a laugh designed to reach them, and Amber glanced towards her, frowning slightly as if suddenly unsure. Instinctively he wanted to wipe away that unsureness.

"I'll check my schedule and see if I'm free." He knew he was, but wanted to buy time. "So tell me all there is to know about them, so I can be prepared."

She laughed. "No preparation required. It's not a meeting, you know. There's no agenda, no action points."

He heard laughter but this time he realized it was coming from him. It felt good. "So you may *think*; you might just find minutes circulated after the event."

"Jeez, I hope not. I wouldn't know what to do with them."

"Ignoring them is best. Now, I need to know, will all the

men in your family be like Gabe and scowl at me? Will they look at me as if they want to castrate me?"

She laughed. "Yes, probably. But don't worry, us girls will look after you. There's Lizzi who's coming up from Shelter Springs, she runs a café there with her husband and has just had her second child... my nephew. And..."

David sighed, and the breath held a mixture of bemusement at such a large family, irritation that he was forced to meet them, and something far more strange, something which he could only name as contentment as he listened to Amber describe her family.

He was annoyed with Katherine for making Amber doubt herself. They were like opposite ends of the spectrum: Katherine all mind, using her body like a tool for her mind, and Amber all heart. He'd once thought he could do without heart. But since his sister's accident he knew better.

"You're doing it again, David."

"What?" he asked, startled out of his reverie.

"You're not listening to me."

"Of course I am. I've been"—he hesitated, feeling uncharacteristically flummoxed, although he knew from experience that he wouldn't show it—"listening to *everything* you've been saying. I haven't missed a word."

"Really?"

"Yes, really." And he hadn't. Years of negotiation where he'd had to pick up the subtext of a discussion had made him adept at both listening and observing. "Why would you think I wasn't listening to you?"

"Well, for starters, I very much doubt that the ins and outs of my world is of any interest to you."

He didn't move or speak, stunned by how absolutely wrong she was. He hadn't intended to find her interesting, hadn't prepared for it in the least. Maybe that was where he'd gone wrong. He usually prepared for every eventuality. It was, he'd always considered, the secret to his success. But somehow everything she said and did found its place within him. The silence stretched but still he couldn't find the words to reassure her without revealing his feelings. He wasn't even sure what those feelings were, nor how to express them. So he stayed silent.

She pressed her lips together and shrugged and a shadow dimmed her brightness momentarily. "It's okay. I'm not sure many people listen to me. I think most people find me a joke." Her lips twitched as if trying to smile but failing. Her gaze flickered away from him and she looked around, as her hand sought her bag, the candlelight glancing off its sequins and showering her face with sparkling light. He felt an unaccountable pain in that place where he'd felt something slot into place. He'd come to think of it as the Amber place. With surprise, he realized he was feeling her pain.

"I think I'd better leave," she said.

He reached out and took her hand. "Amber, you're no joke to me. You have to believe that."

"I do."

"You do? You don't doubt me?"

"No," she said. "I know you're always serious about everything. Someone who gives such serious consideration to a café menu which never changes from one week to the next, isn't likely to be flakey about deciding to take someone to dinner."

He smiled. "Well, I'm glad you realize I'm not flakey." He didn't think that word had ever been used in connection with him in his whole life—there had never been a necessity to describe him as its opposite.

"No, you're serious, but I'm not sure why."

"Because I like you. I really like you."

Amber glanced at Katherine, who had risen to leave with her partner and wiggled her fingers their way. She nodded in response and turned back to face him. "But not in the way you liked Katherine. I can tell."

He sat back with a sigh. "Amber, you and I have nothing to do with Katherine. I suggest you forget about her."

"She's hard to forget," mumbled Amber, and he followed her gaze to where Katherine was drawing attention to herself as she walked out of the restaurant. He could feel Amber drifting away from him. That would never do. Desperate times called for desperate measures.

"I'd like to see you again, Amber. Really, I would."

"Then come to my family dinner."

Even while he drew in a long breath like a dying man, scared of drowning, he knew that there was only one way to get what he wanted.

"Sure." He tried to smile but he wasn't sure his mouth complied. "I'll rearrange my schedule. I'll make sure I can come."

He was rewarded with a beaming smile. "Wonderful! I'm sure you won't regret it. My family are all just lovely."

Just lovely, he repeated to himself with a sigh.

4

*D*avid looked across at the old building and shook his head. The faulty brickwork, which was there for everyone to see, was the least of the structural problems. The earthquake had made the 130-year-old building a death trap. Shame other people refused to see it that way. From his vantage point in the ultra modern offices across the road he could see the cracks radiating out from the windows where the boney old lime mortar had crumbled, threatening the integrity of the old double-brick building. Another shake and David was convinced it would be reduced to rubble.

Angus, his business partner, came and stood beside him and followed his gaze. "Someone told me the other day that we should strengthen it—repoint the mortar, add steel structure within the building to reinforce the whole thing." He swore under his breath. "I told him not to waste his breath. That we didn't operate like that."

"If we spent on it what it was worth, it wouldn't see out the next earthquake. And I'm not having any building of mine come crashing down on innocent men, women and children."

Angus turned to him, sympathy in his eyes. David hated sympathy and hated the fact he'd given himself away yet again.

"You can't turn the clock back, David. You can't help Zoe now."

Maybe not, but he could try to alleviate the guilt, which was his constant companion since the accident. It should have been him in that building, not Zoe.

"No, but I can damn well make sure that it never happens to anyone else." He jerked his head to the old building opposite, which had only just withstood the last major earthquake in Christchurch. "That building is coming down and I don't care how many demonstrations we have to call the cops in for, how many rainbows we have to remove." He sighed at the thought of the new rainbow which had popped up, seemingly overnight. He glanced at it now—the colors were beautiful. No bright primaries this time but muted shades drifting into each other like the subtle colors of a slowing growing sunset until the outer edges flared to deepest red.

"They must have got someone else to paint them instead of that red-headed girl. It looks different this time. The colors are different."

David scanned his emails and closed the laptop with a definitive snap.

"No, it's the same artist."

"How do you know?"

"I saw her working on it."

"And you didn't stop her?"

"There was no point." David glanced at the rainbow. Amber must have used a ladder to reach the top of the wall, knowing it could be seen from any angle, including the head office of the development company over the road. He came and stood beside Angus once more.

"And why's that?"

"Because she'd simply come back tomorrow, when I'm not here, and repeat the process." He turned to Angus. "No, this requires a different approach."

"And what's that?"

"A subtle one."

Angus grunted a cynical laugh. "Subtle? You? That's never exactly been your forte, David."

"Maybe not. But I'm working on it." He scooped up his phone from the table and walked to the door. "See you later."

He left the building, as he usually did, through the basement where he got into his car. He exited the narrow alley and then drove directly onto the motorway. There was no public access, so privacy had easily been retained. No one knew of his association with the property company which was knocking down so many of the old inner city buildings, replacing them with modern works of art.

He didn't care for publicity, and he especially didn't care for Amber Connelly to know what he did for a living. It would jeopardize everything. First, he needed her to convince EarthFoods to stop creating adverse publicity to his demolition plans and accept the relocation to a modern commercial complex in the suburbs. Then, well, it would all be over anyway. He'd have what he wanted—a secure building which would ensure there would be no repeat of the disaster which had ended up with his sister becoming paralyzed from the waist down and confined to a wheelchair for the rest of her life.

He'd hoped the council would write it off for demolition, but it seemed it didn't meet their criteria. Which, in David's opinion, was far too wide. David couldn't look at any of these old buildings without a feeling of nausea and dread filling him. He'd step in if he had to, if the council's regulations didn't allow them to demolish. If that meant treading on a few toes, lying by omission, then so be it. It was a small price to pay.

∾

"HERE HE IS!" exclaimed Jim, too heartily. Everyone turned around to see David slam the car door and walk toward the veranda steps. Jim stepped forward and greeted David with a shake of the hand. "Good to see you, David. Now, let me introduce you to everybody."

Everyone turned to look at David who, Amber thought, looked exceptionally handsome in his white shirt and stone-colored chinos. Smarter than any of her brothers and with a machismo to rival even Max, who wore his manliness like a badge of honor. David didn't alter his stance or respond in any way to Max's physical challenge. Most men did. Amber liked it that David didn't feel the need. Max took a step forward and Amber tried to move between them, but the table was in the way.

But, before Max could reach David and any intimidation could occur, Max's wife, Laura, jumped in front and extended her hand to David.

"David!" said Laura. "How lovely to meet you. We've heard all about you from Amber."

Laura momentarily turned her brilliant smile from David to Amber, winked, and then turned to David once more. Amber loved that Laura was watching out for her, trying to smooth the way between Amber's over-protective brothers and David. But Laura was totally gorgeous—blonde, sexy, and fun—and Amber definitely felt in her shade.

But, apart from returning Laura's polite greeting, David didn't seem to pay her much attention. Instead, he followed

Laura's gaze to Amber and smiled. Amber smiled back and sighed as the warmth of his expression filled every inch of her. It wasn't until Gabe cleared his throat and then nudged her that she realized someone had been talking and neither of them had heard.

"David!" she said. A path suddenly cleared in front of her. He stepped forward and took her hand. "Thanks for coming."

"My pleasure." He kissed her cheek. She blushed, and her siblings tried not to grin. "You look beautiful."

She tucked her hair behind her ear and shook her head. She wished he didn't feel he had to say that. She hardly looked beautiful compared to the rest of the women in her family. Still, it was a nice thing to say. "Thank you." She picked up a plate to offer David. "It's sweet of you to say so, but I think the other Connelly women have cornered the market on beauty." She smiled again, but David didn't. He simply glared at the rest of her family. Amber's smile dropped. She hoped no one would notice. As much as she appreciated David's comment, she really didn't want her family upset.

"Would you like a drink?"

"Sure, thank you."

"We have pretty much anything you could want," said Lizzi, the eldest of the family, who ran a café in Shelter Springs, in the Mackenzie country. "Pete brought his latest vintage to top up Pop's collection." She gestured to the wine fridge, which took up one corner of the covered veranda, and which contained a selection of wines from her husband Pete's winery. "So we won't go short, that's for sure."

"Water, please."

"Oh," said Pete, looking crestfallen. He and Lizzi exchanged bewildered looks. Their lives revolved around food and wine, and they didn't understand David's spartan tastes. Which wasn't surprising, because Amber didn't either. All she knew was that there was something quite exciting about watching someone rein himself in that tight. It made you wonder what passions lurked beneath which required such control.

She reached for her own glass of sparkling water and took a gulp. Luckily the moment of silence was broken by the entrance of her other sister, Rachel, who stepped out from the kitchen holding a hot tray in her designer oven gloves.

Just as well she wasn't the insecure type, thought Amber. Because between her sisters-in-law—Maddy and Laura—and her two sisters—Lizzi and Rachel—she didn't stand a chance. Luckily, they were all happily married.

Rachel deposited the hot tray on the table and stood back with a beaming smile. After a day spent in a kitchen, Rachel really shouldn't look quite as fresh and glamorous as she did. She was dressed in a figure-hugging red dress with a deep neckline which showed off her figure. And the only lock of hair out of place looked as if it had been arranged that way for aesthetic reasons—or at least reasons which gave her husband, Zane, an excuse to push it off her face with a loving caress.

Amber shot another glance at David to see if he was checking out Rachel's cleavage—something which Amber had not a chance of possessing, given the size of her boobs—but, again, David appeared the perfect gentleman, saying something polite to Rachel before turning to Zane, to talk about rugby.

It looked like David was passing the first test—not to be distracted by the beauty and charm of the Connelly women. Which would stand him in good stead for the second test—not to be scared off by the Connelly men, who most assuredly would not appreciate David ogling their wives.

"So, what is it you do, David?" asked Max, taking a swig of his beer straight from the bottle before fixing David with an unflinching gaze.

Amber frowned at Max. Max ignored her, *and* the warning hiss from Laura. But, much to Amber's relief, David didn't turn a hair. He faced Max, looking as cool and relaxed as if he were ordering a drink at a bar. "I'm in property development."

Amber's frown dissolved as she became interested. She hadn't known this. She'd thought he was something to do with Finance. Finance with a capital 'F' because it was a thing about which she knew nothing. Come to think about it, she only had vague notions about what a property developer did, too.

"How do you mean, developing? You mean renovating or something?" she asked. She shot him a smile. It seemed like they had more in common than she'd imagined. "I love renovating old houses."

Did she imagine it or did his smile fix a little? "No, more like building new ones."

"Oh, did you build that one opposite Flo's place? The one I saw you going into the other day?"

"Yes, I did."

It was Jim's turn to frown. "The one where old Briar Cottage used to stand? Shame. There was a lot of history in that cottage."

"Not enough to keep it standing unfortunately, sir." Jim's frown deepened at being called 'sir' again. "It was riddled with rot and woodworm. It wasn't cost effective to restore it."

"Must everything come down to cost these days?" exclaimed Jim, his white bushy eyebrows beetling over irritated eyes.

"Yes," said David firmly. "It must." Amber shuffled

forward, trying to wedge herself between David and Jim. This conversation wasn't going as she'd planned. "Otherwise there would be no money to invest in new projects, and there'd be no progress."

"More drinks, anybody?" she called out too loudly, considering she was standing so close to her father and David. They both looked at her with puzzled expressions. "And while I'm getting them, David, let me introduce you to Gabe and Maddy." She laughed nervously. "I forgot. You know them already from the café, don't you?"

Gabe stepped forward with that charisma he had—a warm doctor's presence—which was entirely natural to him. The entire female population—young and old—of Akaroa had gone into mourning when he'd fallen in love and married the mysterious Madeleine, mysterious no longer.

"Good to meet you somewhere different from the café, David. And thank God you got around to asking Amber out. Between my lovely wife and Amber, I began to think I'd ask you out myself if you didn't hurry up."

David's lips tweaked, which Amber took to be a sign of amusement.

"I would have said no, Gabe. You're not my type." The others laughed. "Actually," he said, looking at Amber with a smile, "nor is Amber." The laughter stopped, replaced by a stunned silence. "And yet I was entranced from the moment I saw her. I didn't ask her out immediately because I wanted to see if that interest waned. But..." He sighed and Amber could virtually feel her family leaning in toward him, their anxiety palpable as to what he might say next. "But it didn't. It only increased. She's a beautiful woman with a big heart."

There were huffs, murmurs, and nods of relief from her family.

"You'll be staying for dinner, I hope?" asked Rachel, obviously warmed by his comments. Since Rachel had returned to Akaroa a few years ago, Amber had grown close to the sister she'd barely known before Rachel had departed to make her career as a TV chef. Rachel gave a quick nod of approval to Amber.

"I'm afraid not. I have commitments in Christchurch I can't get out of." His gaze shifted to Amber. "But I couldn't resist Amber's invitation to meet you all."

Suddenly there was jostling and chatter from young voices, and Rachel's daughter Etta and Lizzi's daughter Aimee appeared carrying large trays. Aimee's continuous chatter was punctuated by Etta's odd dry, and to the point, comments. Aimee adored her newly found cousin, thinking her the epitome of cool.

"Careful, Etta," said Zane, steadying the plate just in time before it fell off the edge of the table. Etta was more accomplished at scoring a try in her beloved rugby than waiting at table.

"So," said Jim, clearing his throat. Here it comes, thought Amber. "Do you plan to stay around Akaroa? Is this a permanent or temporary move?"

"Dad!" exclaimed Amber. "That's David's business."

"And it's mine now, since he's shown an interest in you."

"That's okay, Amber. I understand your family is protective of you, and that's as it should be." He turned to Jim Connelly—the family patriarch. "It's temporary."

Amber felt her heart drop and it must have showed in her face.

"For now," he said, looking at her. She gave a wan smile.

"Anyone like a top up?" She held up a bottle of wine, and wandered off, digesting this piece of information. Did she really want to get involved with someone who was passing through? One look at David, now talking to Jim and Pete about property prices in Central Otago, told her that she shouldn't, but that she would.

Lizzi held out her half-empty glass for Amber to refill and nodded toward David. "Trial by Connelly," she muttered. "He's done well to survive us this far."

"He seems pretty solid to me," said Max, with grudging respect, coming up behind Amber and Lizzi and following their gaze to David.

"Solid?" asks Lizzi. "Not sure that demolishing a beautiful old cottage could be called solid. But he seems a nice guy despite that. And *really* interested in you, Amber." Lizzi nudged Amber with her elbow.

Amber felt herself blush. "He does, doesn't he?" she whispered to Lizzi.

"You're wrong, Lizzi," said Max. "Not about his interest in Amber. Of course he is, who wouldn't be?" He gave Amber a quick hug. "You're wrong about demolishing the cottage. What could be more solid than demolishing a rickety old cottage and putting something in its place which will last another couple of centuries? Nothing wrong with that. Nothing to be gained by clinging to old things."

Laura jumped up and came and stood in front of Max, sliding her hands up his chest and around his neck in one sinuous movement. His expression changed immediately.

"Are you saying, Max Connelly," said his beautiful wife, her sexy brief top and tight jeans vying with her bright, mischievous expression to entrance her husband, "that clinging to old things is bad?"

It looked as if Max hadn't a clue what he'd been saying only a few minutes earlier. "I might have been."

"And who is it, dearest husband, who has insisted on keeping the old lanterns at the Lodge because they remind you of your mother?"

Max had the grace to look a bit sheepish. He cleared his

throat as if to rid himself of the weakness. It didn't work. "It could have been me."

"It *was* you. Just as it was you who refused to allow anyone to revamp your man cave into something vaguely resembling clean and modern lines."

"There's nothing wrong with it."

"Nothing that a bomb wouldn't rectify."

"Laura," said Max in a low voice.

"Max," said Laura, echoing his threat and trumping it. She squeaked in surprise as he caught her in his arms and stopped any further talk with a devastating kiss.

His sisters groaned, and Gabe and his two brothers-in-law—Zane and Pete—laughed and shook their heads.

When eventually they parted, Max couldn't take his eyes off Laura.

"I reckon it's time to go."

"No way!" Laura grinned. "I've been promised a swim, and a swim is what I'm going to get before we head back to Queenstown." She turned to the others. "Are you guys going to join me?"

"Not us," said Rachel. "We've got to be back at the marae by seven. Summoned by Zane's mum. Besides, Laura, it's winter, it'll be cold."

"It's practically spring, and it's never very cold."

"So says the girl who won't refuse a dare," said Lizzi with a grin.

Laura grabbed hold of Max's hand so he couldn't escape —not that he looked like he wanted to, thought Amber—and they disappeared around the corner of the house, ducking under the old lantern which was half submerged by the overgrown wisteria, toward the beach.

Lizzi and Rachel took some empty dishes into the kitchen, leaving Pete and Zane with Amber, and Gabe and Maddy talking to David, with Gabe admirably smoothing things between Jim and David.

Zane stretched out in his chair. "Jeez, old Max sure is under his wife's thumb! What do you reckon, Pete?"

Amber shook her head. "You two! You only talk like that when your wives aren't around." Zane grinned, and Amber knew he was joking. She always seemed to take the bait.

Pete laughed and topped up Zane's outstretched wine glass. "Yeah! Who'd have thought it? Doesn't seem two minutes since Max and I were having mates' weekends in the bush. Dropped in the middle of nowhere, just a few of us—accountable to no one—and then a weekend of hunting and drinking."

"Drinking?" exclaimed Lizzi, as she and Rachel came through from the kitchen. She snagged Pete's glass from him and finished it off and handed him back the empty glass. "Aimee asked if you could read her a story."

Pete looked from his empty wine glass to Lizzi and then back to Zane and shrugged.

Zane laughed until Rachel did the exact same thing. She drained the glass and put it on the table with a broad grin. She extended her hand. "Time to go, Zane. We've got a walk ahead of us yet."

Zane didn't look Pete in the eye, and Amber noticed Pete also mumbled something about Aimee wanting him. So much for her macho brothers-in-law. The Connelly women won out every time. She looked at David. The thought gave her hope for what she was about to do.

She'd bide her time, though. David had said he couldn't stay long, but she was determined to make every second count. She walked over to the remaining group and David welcomed her with a warm smile and a side step to make room for her. She felt very feminine and nurtured as a brief silence fell, as everyone noted the warmth of David's gaze on Amber, a warmth which he didn't demonstrate with anyone else. It was nice, thought Amber, smiling up at him. Very nice. She could get used to this.

"Let me show you the beach, David. We're lucky enough to have our own private beach at Belendroit."

"Ah, Lantern Bay. It always looks so picturesque from town, especially at night, lit by the lanterns around your house."

"It's even better close to."

David glanced at Jim. "If you'll excuse me, sir."

"Please, call me Jim. And, yes, you go and see the beach. It's beautiful. My wife and I used to spend most of our time there. And the kids when they were younger…" He sighed as he became lost in memories, and Amber gave him a hug and a peck on the cheek.

"Pop, don't go feeling sorry for yourself. A day doesn't go by without someone coming to visit."

Jim's eyes brightened. "It's certainly been lovely having Etta and all her friends visit. And when you marry and have children…" He broke off, as if suddenly aware of the situation.

Amber cleared her throat and shot her father a meaningful look. "See you later, Pop!"

"Come on," she said to David with a smile. With Gabe and Maddy following, they went around the corner and walked across the increasingly springy grass until they reached the shoreline. A jetty went into the water and they were in time to see Etta jump off, doing a star jump against the darkening sky, then falling with a splash. Like Laura, Etta wasn't afraid of cold water.

Amber sat on an upturned boat and David sat beside her. When Maddy and Gabe sat on the end of the dock watching the swimmers, they were alone.

For a moment David watched Amber's family splashing and laughing in the sea, then he moved his serious gaze to the beauty of the dark hills which surrounded the harbor and the indigo sky still bright enough to reveal the shredded remnants of the sunset. Then his gaze settled on the lanterns which were strewn around the property, encompassing it with a light and security which never failed to move Amber. But, rather than look happy, David's face grew more grim. He blinked. She'd thought he'd like it. Lantern Bay was one of her most favorite spots in the world.

"Is everything all right? I'm afraid my family can be a bit full-on."

He turned to her and shrugged. "No, they're fine. I mean, they're very nice. I didn't find them full-on at all."

Amber grunted and toed the sand. It was no doubt true, because David was pretty full on himself. But she liked that. She was so easygoing that people often overlooked her. She always admired people who couldn't be overlooked, people who stood midstream in a strong current of life while everything had to move around them. She was more likely to float off on the current. She sighed.

"Why the sigh?" David asked. And she turned to see he was closer to her, his face shadowy against the lantern which dangled from the pohutukawa tree behind him. "It sounded very wistful."

"I was just thinking about how you are with them." She shrugged. "With everybody really."

"And how is that?"

"Uncompromising, I guess."

"Is that a bad thing?"

"Not good, or bad. Just a thing. It's certainly a thing which would give you what you want more easily."

He nodded. "You should try it."

She shrugged again and looked out at her sister-in-law and niece splashing in the bay. "I like a quiet life. I don't think going after what I want would bring me that."

"Why? What is it you want?"

"Nothing much."

"Come on. Close your eyes and tell me what would make you happy."

She laughed, but closed her eyes and let her thoughts drift and form images of things which would bring her joy. "An exhibition of my paintings. A proper one. Not like the craft exhibition where you bought my paintings. But like a proper exhibition with only my paintings shown. A successful exhibition where all my paintings are sold." She opened her eyes. "But that's just vanity."

"Nothing wrong with vanity. Why don't you organize one?"

"No one is interested."

"What about your café? I'd have thought that would be the perfect venue. People go there because of you, because the café is all about your personality."

"Really?"

"Yes, really."

Amber grunted. "I hadn't thought of it like that. Anyway, I *have* asked them, but they prefer to show the touristy things."

"Leave it with me. I have some contacts." It was nice of him, but she was under no illusions he'd be successful. "What else?"

She closed her eyes. And for some reason, the Eiffel Tower popped into her head. She opened her eyes again. "Nothing else. Just be happy with what I'm doing here, in Akaroa."

"You've really no thoughts outside this place? You've never been interested in any other country?"

"Oh, I love all things French. But then, in Akaroa, we have French history, so…"

"But what about travel? Presumably you've been to Europe?"

She shook her head. "No."

"So... where have you been?"

"Nowhere. Just here. Sometimes I go to Shelter Springs to see Lizzi, but otherwise I stay in Akaroa and Christchurch."

"Why don't you travel?"

Why indeed? How had he managed to drive the conversation to this? The memories of what happened five years ago were still vivid. She could feel the visceral clenching in her gut. She swallowed, suddenly nervous.

"I don't like to."

"But you'd love France. I can just picture you there. You'd love everything about it. And not just France. What about Italy? Morocco? Berlin?"

She gave a tight smile and shook her head. She jumped up. "We should be getting back. Pop will be feeling left out."

But before she could turn around, David laid his hand on her arm. It was only a light touch, but it stilled her. She turned to face him and found him nearer than she'd imagined.

He brushed his fingers against her cheek. "What is it? What makes you suddenly so afraid? It's only the world."

"Maybe the world isn't to be trusted?" She shrugged again and walked away, ignoring his light touch on her arm. She quickened her pace and was soon away from the beach, back under the veranda lights with her father sitting in his usual chair reading the paper. This was what she wanted. Security. Safety.

He looked over his glasses at her. "No swim for you this evening, Amber?"

She was so choked up she couldn't bring herself to reply. Just shook her head.

He frowned. "Is everything all right?"

"Of course. Why wouldn't it be?"

"Is David—"

But whatever her father had been about to say was lost as David came round the corner.

"It's all fine, Pop, honestly. David's about to leave."

But, as Amber stepped away to allow David and her father to say their goodbyes—both obviously still wary of each other—Amber couldn't help thinking that things weren't just fine. Being with David, talking with David, was stirring up things she'd prefer to forget, challenging things she'd decided were the only way forward. Life was easier staying within known boundaries, known limits, where she couldn't be hurt. Suddenly she realized that both David and her father were looking at her.

"Sorry?" she asked.

"I was just saying, Amber," said Jim, as David walked down the steps towards her, "that David must come again."

"Of course. That would be lovely."

David and Amber walked across the shadowy lane to where he'd parked his car. She leaned against the rear door as he opened his door.

"Thank you for inviting me, Amber. I've enjoyed meeting your family." He cast a quick glance at Jim, who immediately turned away. They were being observed, and both David and Amber knew it. They looked back at each other with a smile.

"Sorry about Max. I think he still believes I'm twelve years old and need protecting."

"That's fair enough. You are his little sister and you always will be. A brother should protect his sister."

"Maybe, but he's not here to protect me now." She took a step closer, because it didn't look as if he would. And without another word—because what else was left to say?—she slid her hands over his shoulders, rolled onto tiptoes and pressed her lips against his. For a fraction of a moment, when he began to answer her kiss and it deepened, she thought she'd fallen into a place where she belonged. Then he gripped her around her upper arm and stepped away. She didn't know who was more embarrassed.

They both began to speak at once and stopped at once.

"I'm sorry, I thought…" She shook her head. "Never mind." She turned and ran away a few steps before turning back to see that he hadn't moved. "My mistake." She paused to give him a chance to speak. It was dark where he'd parked amongst the trees, and the lights from the lanterns didn't extend far enough to reveal his expression—only his outline: hands on hips, white shirt glowing in the dark. His dark hair and dark eyes revealed no reaction. "Right, I…" She trailed off, nodding toward the house. "Goodnight, then," she mumbled, before turning and walking quickly back to the house.

Even at the house, as she slowed her walk and climbed the steps onto the now empty veranda, she thought he might follow her any moment and explain why he hadn't kissed her back. But all she heard was the roar of his engine, and all she saw were its tail lights as it bounced over the rutted drive and out onto the winding coast road, back to Akaroa.

Why didn't David want her? Was there something wrong with her?

"Amber!" Jim's voice brought back to the present with an abrupt bump.

She followed his voice into the library where Jim—who'd obviously had a hefty slug of his replenished tumbler of whiskey in the time Amber had gone to the car—was looking at old photos. He had one of them in his hand, and the whiskey in the other. "Lizzi looks so like your mother."

Amber took the photo from him. "Ah, look at us all." Her eyes lingered on her mother—who had died when she was only eleven—and then Lizzi. "Even then they looked like sisters."

He put the photo back. "It was before she became ill. She was a beautiful woman. I didn't deserve her."

"Oh, Pop. That's the alcohol talking." She took his half-finished whiskey and placed it on the sideboard. "We're still here for you. Look at us all tonight."

She managed to put a smile on his face. "That's true." Then he laughed. "It certainly wasn't boring with your David there."

"What do you mean?" Amber asked.

"Seems to me," said Jim, "that your David—"

"Not *my* David," said Amber sulkily, remembering the rebuffed kiss.

"Well, he's not mine!" he said, shooting her an outraged look. "As I was saying, I think your David created more confusion than anyone you've ever brought here." He retrieved his whiskey and took a generous slug, grimacing slightly. "Or *anyone* has ever brought here." He placed his glass a little too firmly onto the table. "Rachel looked insulted at his response to her dinner."

"He has some kind of prior engagement."

"What?"

"I don't know."

"And he didn't eat any of Rachel's fancy baking."

"I guess he doesn't eat that kind of food."

"It's wonderful food."

"I guess he doesn't eat *wonderful* food then."

"He doesn't drink wine, so Pete didn't have anything to talk to him about."

"He talked to Lizzi," she said.

"Correction. Lizzi talked to him, while his eyes followed you around the room."

She flushed pink at the thought. "Did they?" Suddenly all the doubts and concerns about the evening vanished.

"Yep," said Jim. "They sure did. Your David managed to

confuse, bewilder, upset and aggravate everyone to some degree or other."

Amber sighed. Her dad was right because it sure felt he'd done all of those things to her. Trouble was he'd also charmed the hell out of her. And she didn't know what on earth she was going to do about that.

5

*A*mber lay in her small bedroom at Belendroit watching the sunlight filter through the leaves, creating dancing shadows on the ceiling rose, and catching the crystal droplets of the chandelier with sudden sparkles of color. Her father said the elaborate chandelier looked incongruous in such a small room. It had been hers since birth, and despite having her own cottage in town, she still often used it. More to keep her father company, she'd always persuaded herself. But now she was beginning to wonder.

David's direct questions about traveling forced her to confront the real reason why she never went anywhere. She was plain scared. After what had happened to her, she'd been more than happy to do as her father had suggested—stay close to home. Stay away from anyone who might take her away and use her, taking advantage of her nature which was to sail away, like a leaf on the water, like a cloud scudding across the sky. She wanted to be anchored here, where it was safe.

But she trusted David. And, for the first time in years, she imagined spreading her wings with David by her side. It was a happy thought.

⁓

"SOMEONE LOOKS HAPPY," said Flo, glancing up from her paperwork.

"Yes," said Amber, tossing down her tasseled, beflowered handbag she'd bought for a song at a flea market in Christchurch. "Someone is."

Flo grinned, sat back and studied Amber. "I wonder if that's something to do with a certain David I've been hearing so much about."

Amber sat down, flung her arms wide and slid them along the antimacassars which Flo had kept from her grandparents' day. "I'm in love, Flo!"

"Oh no," Flo groaned. "With David? I mean, I hear he's a nice guy and all, but isn't he meant to be some kind of cutthroat property dealer?"

Amber frowned. "Who have you been talking to?"

Flo shrugged, obviously trying to hide the person's identity, but Amber knew it could have been any one of a number of people. David's personality wasn't the kind to make instant friends. She sighed. "I'm sure he's not cutthroat, but he does do something with property."

"Oh well. I guess doing things with property doesn't make people intrinsically evil!" She grinned. "So tell me about this David. I've heard he's been seen in and around Akaroa a lot recently. Is he chasing you?"

Amber opened her mouth to reply but closed it again. She grimaced. "I don't think so. I think it's more the other way around."

"What?"

Amber nibbled her fingernails and then stared at them.

"Yes, I tried to kiss him yesterday, but he didn't seem to have any interest in kissing me back. He walked away instead."

Flo crossed her arms and leaned back against the kitchen bench. "I don't like the sound of that! Why wouldn't he kiss you?"

Amber grimaced. "I guess… I guess, I'm not really his type. He's so different to me."

"And yet you say you love him."

"Oh, Flo, I really think I do. It doesn't matter that things don't make sense in my head. Whenever I'm near him, I just melt." She sighed. "He's totally gorgeous, and he's all I can think about."

"Wait, let me get this right. You love him, want him, and he's all you think about, but he doesn't seem that interested in you?"

Amber screwed up her face as she tried to put the contradiction she felt in him into words. "He kind of does seem interested on one hand, but on the other he runs a mile at the first sign of intimacy. I can't fathom it out."

Flo came over and sat on the coffee table opposite Amber. "Please, do me a favor, Amber. Don't lose your heart to this guy unless he's going to lose his to you. I can't bear the thought of you falling for another guy who is Trouble. And that's Trouble with a capital T."

"This isn't like last time."

"Are you sure?"

"He's not a sleaze. Not like, you know." She couldn't bring herself to name the guy who'd brought her so much grief. "He was clear right from the beginning what he wanted."

Flo glowered. "Shame it was you."

"Yep," said Amber, pressing her lips together in regret.

"So," Flo sighed, sitting back. "He's not a sleaze… that's good. A definite improvement. And he seems to be interested, and yet you're not totally sure."

"That about sums it up."

"Then do me a favor, find out for sure if he's interested in you before you totally lose your heart to this guy. I don't want you hurt again. None of us do."

"Sure," said Amber, jumping to her feet. She went and looked over Flo's shoulder. "So what are you up to? Paperwork?"

Flo waved the papers triumphantly. "A contract! My new solicitor has come up trumps with finding me funding for the house."

"Really? Wow, that's just what you've been wanting."

"I know. Maddy helped so much by providing me with a regular flow of guests, but I need investment. And it looks like I've found it."

"Who is the investor?"

Flo shrugged. "Some anonymous finance company who sees the potential in Akaroa and is happy to fund me with the lowest interest rate around."

"Oh," said Amber, doubtfully. Even to her unbusiness-like ears, it sounded odd. "What's in it for them?"

"My solicitor said that the company wants to preserve Akaroa's heritage buildings."

Amber grunted. "I wish they owned our EarthFoods building. Anyway"—she kissed Flo on the cheek—"I'd better go, mouths to feed, the public to greet, a café to run."

Amber left the house thinking it was already too late not to lose her heart. That horse had already bolted. But, still, it wouldn't hurt to do as Flo suggested—to find out whether David really was interested in her—because Amber sure was curious.

A FEW DAYS LATER, across the other end of the peninsula, in a central Christchurch gym, David was trying to work off his bad mood. He'd hardly had any sleep the last few nights because all he could think about was Amber. Max had been right to warn him off. He had no right flirting with her, knowing that there was no future. Trouble was, he was falling for her. When she'd leaned over and kissed him, it was all he could do to move away.

And seeing that unexpected fear in her eyes, when she'd talked about what she wanted, had brought out that part of him which hated to see people afraid. It was the same with his sister—he'd do, and had done, anything to make sure her life was happy. There was a part of him which was too noble for his own good. He wanted to set the worlds to rights, beginning with his sister and then working outwards, saving everyone, one person at a time.

He wiped his face, slammed the towel onto the bench, stripped off his clothes and got under the cold shower, waiting for the freezing pricks of ice to numb his senses. Unfortunately, they only went skin deep.

His mood hadn't lightened by the time he reached the office. After receiving a telling off from his sister, David finished the call with a glower. He loved his sister dearly, but he really could do without her nagging him.

He'd made the mistake of telling her about Amber. He always told Zoe everything but had intended to keep Amber to himself. But every minute he spent with Amber, he became more involved and so had ended up telling Zoe about her. Including his reluctance to take it further. He drew the line as to why he didn't want to take it further. He didn't want his sister to know quite how devious he'd become in the pursuit of his obsession to demolish every potentially dangerous building in the city.

Telling Zoe about Amber had proved a big mistake. She'd

asked to meet her; he'd refused. But he suspected Zoe had already gone to the café to check Amber out because Zoe had told David in no uncertain terms that he'd better not mess this one up. David was still gritting his teeth with annoyance when his partner, Angus, strode in and went to the window.

"They are there again. Bloody nuisances! I thought you said you had a plan to stop them. If you have, it's not bloody working!"

David walked up behind Angus and followed his angry gaze to the old building opposite, its dark, cracked exterior enlivened with rainbows and other fey motifs. Outside the shop, baskets lined the pavement like an old-fashioned greengrocers. He could almost catch the earthy whiff of organic grains and seeds from here. He sighed as his gaze shifted to the woman who was single-handedly painting a rainbow over the black paint, which they'd only just finished applying to eradicate her previous painting. Her red hair was as vivid as the rainbow.

Angus grabbed his phone and strode to the door. "I'm going to go and have it out with her! She's a bloody menace. Her and the rest of them."

"No!" said David. "I'll do it."

"You keep saying you have it in hand. But it doesn't look like it to me."

"Believe me. I do. It'll be less messy, there will be less publicity, if we persuade her to stop. She's the major shareholder in the co-operative. Get her on our side and the rest will follow. They'll have no other choice."

"And how exactly do you propose to do that? I suppose its using your legendary chick-magnet charm?" Angus groaned. "You do. You plan to seduce her, don't you? Don't you think she'll be able to see through you?"

David shook his head. "No." He looked at Amber.

"Why not? Surely any woman with their usual cynicism could see through you?"

"Not this woman," said David, leaving the office.

"Why not? What makes this woman so different?" called his partner to the closed door.

Because, thought David, she isn't just any woman, and, besides, she didn't have a cynical bone in her body. Which only made it so much worse.

AMBER POKED out her tongue as she concentrated on completing the arc of the rainbow. Other people signed their rainbows, but she didn't. She didn't want to own it, or claim it. As far as she was concerned, it was there to be enjoyed and owned by everybody.

She stepped back and smiled. A thing of beauty once again graced the black paint of the developers. She wished they'd stop, but this seemed to be the best, most beautiful, passive demonstration against their aims. She could keep it up. They'd lose interest before she did.

She suddenly realized how late it was and looked around anxiously. She began to clean her brushes and pack away her things. She wanted to be back in Akaroa by evening. She always hated being away from home, getting anxious and edgy the closer to night it got. With her car still in the garage, she was getting a lift home from one of the shop workers as far as Little River, from where Maddy had said she'd pick Amber up.

"Amber!"

She turned suddenly at the sound of her name. David was walking over to her from his car, parked in front of the building opposite.

"You'll get a fine if you park there," said Amber. "The owners of that building are always doing that."

David raised an eyebrow and glanced around at his car. He turned back to her. "I'll risk it. So," he said, stepping over to her. "How are you?"

"I'm excellent, thank you!" She dropped the last of her paint brushes into her battered wooden box, which she then placed into her woven basket. "What a coincidence to see you here."

David cleared his throat, then opened his mouth, but nothing came out. He shook his head with a surprised huff.

"Is anything the matter?" she said, frowning, approaching him, searching his face. "You look—"

"I'm fine," he interrupted, pushing his fingers through his hair in an uncharacteristically unsure movement. "I saw you here and thought I'd stop to say hello."

"I'm glad you did. And great timing, too. I've just finished." She indicated the rainbow. "What do you think?"

"It's…" He shook his head. "Very"—he shrugged—"colorful."

Her face dropped. "You don't like it."

"It's lovely, but I'm not sure it's in the right place." He looked at her carefully.

"What do you mean? It's in exactly the right place! EarthFoods is being intimidated by the owners of the building to move out! Do you know what they want to do?" She stepped closer, glaring at David, her heart and eyes ablaze with passion at the injustice of it all. She didn't wait for him to reply, which was just as well as it didn't look as if he was going to. "They want to demolish it." Tears shone in her eyes. "They want to tear it down. It's unbelievable, isn't it?" She spread her fingers over the dark-painted stonework. "It was built in 1890, and generations of Christchurch people have lived and worked and shopped and prayed here. How can they do that? Ignore such a rich history of people?"

He shrugged but indicated a place in the brickwork where the masonry had had to be propped up. "Maybe that's a clue?"

She looked from the brickwork back to him, enraged now. "It's a clue as to the dereliction of their duties! That's what it's a clue to. Really, David, I can see you need educating! Have you been inside?"

"No, I haven't." And by his body language, it didn't look as if he wanted to now, either.

She grabbed his hand and pulled him. He remained firm. "No, I don't have time. And I can assure you I don't need educating about buildings. Now, I'm off to Akaroa to have dinner with my sister. I wondered if you'd care for a lift if you're still carless?"

The wind immediately left Amber's sails. The passion of a few moments ago was overtaken by the beguiling thought of being in David's company for an hour, at least.

"That would be lovely. I was getting a lift as far as Little River with Lois from the shop. But she's working late and I prefer to be home before dark."

He smiled. "Before dark? Nervous of the big, bad city, are you?"

She didn't smile. "I'll get my things."

"I'll bring the car over."

She gathered her baskets and paints and jacket and watched as he skillfully maneuvered his car and pulled it into the vacant lot beside the shop. He opened the door for her. It seemed very gallant and old-fashioned.

"Thank you."

As they pulled away, she glanced up to the first floor opposite where the enemies were and she could have sworn she saw a wave aimed at David. But he wasn't looking. He didn't make any sign of recognition. She must have imagined it. They were probably waving dismissively, glad she'd gone for the night.

"So," he said, pulling into the late afternoon traffic flowing out of Christchurch city center. "Apart from painting rainbows, what have you been doing since I last saw you?"

"Working in the café, of course, and then quiet evenings painting."

"Quiet evenings… I like the sound of those."

She looked out the window at the trees fringing the park. It was an exquisitely lit winter afternoon with the encroaching night beginning to make its presence felt, chasing the light away. His voice rumbled against her skin, making her think of the kiss they'd barely had. But she wouldn't think of that.

"I like busy days and quiet evenings. Daylight talking with people, dark on my own, thinking and painting."

He glanced at her with interest, before indicating and smoothly overtaking someone. "And what do you think about on those long dark evenings?"

She held his gaze until he broke it to look ahead at the traffic. "All last week I've been thinking about the last time I saw you. At Belendroit. And I was wondering why you left me in such a hurry."

The smile around his lips faded instantly and she noticed his grip tighten around the steering wheel. Perhaps it wasn't the best place to find out that he didn't like her enough to go out with her. Neither could escape for the hour it would take to reach Akaroa.

"It's okay. You don't need to tell me. You just asked me what I was thinking about, that's all." She sighed into the silence. "Gabe always tells me I'm too honest for my own good."

"Nothing wrong with honesty."

She decided to count to ten and see if he continued. But it seemed he could cope with silence longer than she could.

"Anyway, my painting is coming along well."

"That's great," David said in a very relieved voice, which sunk Amber's heart even further. "When are you going to exhibit them?"

She turned to him, astonished. "Exhibit my work?" She twisted back in her chair and looked ahead. "Chance would be a fine thing. My work isn't the kind of thing which galleries want. It's not commercial enough, it's not high-brow enough, it's not... ever enough."

"That's just marketing. Your work is enough for you and there will be others like you." She wondered if she heard a slight hesitancy as he finished the sentence. "Who," he said with renewed strength in his voice, "would love to own your work. I mean, I own a couple of your paintings."

"They were probably the best ones."

"What are your others like?"

"Different. Would you like to see them?"

"Yes, I would. Very much." Now this he said with a warmth which couldn't be mistaken.

"Very good. Then you shall. When are you expected at your sister's?"

"Anytime. I can text her to say I'll be a bit late."

"Then come for a drink at my place and I'll show you my work."

"That, Amber, sounds like something I would very much like to do."

"Good," she said with a laugh, settling back in the comfort of the near-horizontal leather seat, and wondering at the same time whether David hadn't watched too many Regency dramas growing up. Someone more like Darcy out of *Pride and Prejudice*, she couldn't imagine. But she liked it, which made her wonder if she hadn't spent too much of her youth on re-runs of *Pride and Prejudice* as well. The thought made her smile.

"I like seeing you smile," he said, glancing at her before signaling to overtake.

And Amber couldn't think of a response, because she thought that perhaps that was one of the nicest things a man had ever said to her. It suggested a lack of selfishness and ego on his part which surprised her, coming as it did from a man who, on the surface, appeared to be all about self and ego. And it also suggested an interest which reassured her. Maybe she'd get that kiss after all.

As THE LOW shining red car pulled up outside her small cottage, the neighbors' curtains twitched to check out the unusual noise. David knew why. Amber's parking space was usually occupied by her yellow VW beetle decorated with butterfly transfers, which was a whole lot noisier than David's Jaguar, and half the time it didn't go.

As he got out of the car and Amber exchanged greetings with neighbors on both sides of her cottage, he couldn't help putting himself in their shoes. They'd be wondering what on earth a man like him was doing with a girl like Amber. He knew they'd be thinking that because he was thinking the exact same thing. But he couldn't seem to stop himself.

As Amber chatted easily with the old lady who leaned out of the window to tell Amber her concerns over her missing cat, he couldn't help but be moved by Amber's easy ability to empathize with the woman, and to say exactly the right things to comfort her and to make her more cheerful. The woman, from having a worried face, closed the window with a smile and a wave. Amber seemed to bring light into a world where none existed. And he hadn't the faintest idea how she did it. He could analyze anything but her. She was a total enigma and he couldn't get her out of his mind. Or anywhere else.

She rummaged in her wicker basket—the likes of which he hadn't seen since his grandmother's day—for the keys. At last she found them. How, he didn't know, because they were hidden under a perplexing array of things which he'd have thought would have been better kept in a cupboard somewhere. Preferably not his. She twisted a key, like he'd only ever seen before in a museum, in the lock, and opened the door.

"Welcome to my home," she said proudly.

He took one step and entered a different world. And he knew, in that moment, that it was a world that he didn't want to leave. He shot her a quick smile, glanced at the world outside and wondered briefly how he could ever have thought he could live in that world without the knowledge that this one existed.

Amber closed the door and switched on a side light, then another, then another. Apparently there were no center lights. She stood, looking uncertain but happy, on what appeared to be a rag rug—he only knew because he'd seen one in a colonial museum his sister had dragged him to once —with the warm glow of the lamps creating a halo around her red hair. There was a fireplace behind her, its Victorian surround and cast iron hearth showing remnants of a fire. He shook his head. No fire was needed with Amber there.

She frowned. "Is everything okay? I know it's nothing like you're used to but—"

"It reminds me of my grandmother's house," he blurted out. Memories washed through his mind with all the uncontrollable force of a tsunami. Things he thought he'd forgotten now flashed through his mind. "Anyway," he said quickly, regretting his impulse to say what was on his mind. "These are the paintings, are they?" he asked, pointing to the stack which was piled in a corner.

"Yes, they're my newer ones."

"May I?"

"Sure."

She stood back while he flicked through the pile. They were definitely Amber's, but they were also definitely something different to her usual style. "They're beautiful. They'd look right at home in any of the inner city galleries."

"Yeah, well, that's an option." She walked over to the small kitchen, which was off the back of the only living room. "Would you like a cup of tea, glass of wine or anything?"

"No, thanks."

"Oh. I thought you'd stay for a bit."

"No, I won't."

She put the kettle down and walked up to him. He wished she hadn't. It was all he could do to stop himself from reaching out to her, pushing his fingers through her hair and holding her face steady so he could kiss her as he'd imagined kissing her since he'd met her. He swallowed and clenched his hands. He wouldn't give in.

"That's a shame," she said quietly. "We seem to keep meeting and then you leave, too soon."

"Too soon for what?" he asked. As soon as the words had slipped out, he knew he'd said entirely the wrong thing.

"For this," she said, rolling onto her tiptoes, putting her hands through his hair and holding his head steady, just as he'd imagined doing, and pressing her lips to his.

It was quiet inside the room, cocooned by velvet curtains, thick rugs, and with only the ticking of an antique carriage clock for company. Outside, the sound of wind chimes gathered pace as the rain which had been threatening gently rolled in from the sea.

The feel of her fingers on his head, her breath against his, her tongue teasing his, broke down the last remaining defenses. He put his arms around her and kissed her like he'd wanted to kiss her ever since he'd met her.

Eventually they parted, Amber continuing to kiss his lips and neck, before nestling into his arms with a sigh.

"You're an enigma, Amber," he breathed. "So beautiful, such a part of the world and people, and yet not. And yet you're hiding here, somehow."

"*I'm* an enigma?" She looked up at him with a smile. "I've been trying without success to figure you out since day one. I think I'm pretty much an open book."

He shook his head. "No. You're not." He scanned her face, his fingers tracing her cheekbones, nose and lips, marveling at their delicate contours, the softness of her skin and the kiss that had been so much more than he'd imagined—and he'd imagined a lot. "The more I get to know you, the more I realize there is that I don't understand. You're open and trusting and yet… I don't know. There's a shadow there.

"Shadow?" She grunted. "You're imagining things."

"I have no imagination. You should know that about me by now. No, like back there, in Christchurch, when you'd finished your painting and you realized you were alone, that look of panic on your face. What was that about?"

"Me, panicked? Surely not?" She tried to move out from his embrace, but he held onto her hand.

"Yes, you were. You looked… scared almost. Afraid to meet me on your own?"

She looked up at him with a serious expression, which wiped the encouraging smile from his face.

"No, it was nothing to do with you."

"Then why so scared to be on your own at four thirty on a winter's afternoon in central Christchurch?"

Her smile fell away and pain like a shadow fell over it. She swallowed. "I was sixteen when it happened."

A feeling of dread slid through him. He suddenly felt sick to his stomach. "What?" he barely whispered.

"I met a boy in Christchurch. Just a boy. A lad. A young man in ripped jeans with long hair and a guitar. And I went back to his house." She shrugged.

"What happened?"

She sucked in a breath and he could see that it was hard for her to continue. "I'm sorry, I don't usually tell people."

"It's okay. Take your time."

He took hold of her hands in his and swept his thumbs across them, trying to give her the reassurance and strength it appeared she needed. She smiled and looked at him with such trust that anything that remained of his hardened heart melted.

"He must have spiked my drink. I don't really know. Everything is so hazy."

"When did it stop being hazy?"

"It took five days for me to come round."

"And no one came for you?"

"No one knew I was there. He must have forgotten to top up the drugs one time, and I came around." Her eyes darkened with fear as she remembered the moment. "And I escaped. The police found me wandering the streets, and took me home. I've hardly left there since. Not wanted to. And I only ever visit Christchurch during the day, and I stick to the places I know." She shrugged. "Scared, I guess."

He swore softly under his breath at the thought of this beautiful soul being subjected to the worst kind of violence against a woman. He felt pain in his whole being, from the tip of his fingers to his gut to his chest—everything ached with an unfamiliar pain. He wanted to shout out his anger and frustration that such a thing could happen to someone like Amber—could happen to anyone, but especially the trusting and vulnerable Amber. She was too good for this world, and he wanted to make sure nothing like that happened to her again.

But it was, wasn't it? He had entered her life with the sole purpose of using her to make her stop her peaceful protests, which were proving so disruptive to his development of the building. But he knew, now, that that would have to stop. The building be damned. He'd do anything not to hurt Amber, anything to keep her safe and happy.

He pulled her to him and held her tight against his chest. He placed his cheek against her hair and felt her breath against his chest, her hands moving tentatively around his back, her fingers splaying and pulling him tighter to her. He'd felt an instant connection, despite their very obvious differences, when he'd first seen her. And that connection had deepened with every subsequent meeting. For the first time ever he both wanted her physically— wanted to kiss every square inch of that beautiful pale skin of hers, and her slender limbs, wanted to make love to her —and wanted to connect with her emotionally. But he could do neither until he'd cleared up the mess he'd created for himself. And then, he promised himself, he'd begin again with Amber. But he wouldn't leave without a demonstration of his intent.

He pulled away and gently cupped her face. "I'm so sorry you had to experience something like that. I'm so, so sorry."

"It wasn't your fault," said Amber with a smile.

Maybe, he thought, but he was as guilty as sin for how he'd planned to use her. But that was the past, he told himself firmly. "I promise you that I'll never let anything like that happen to you again."

She shook her head, her beautiful hair shifting beneath his hands. "No. That's what my family try to do—keep me close, keep me safe—but I need to be myself, I need to live and breath and feel free."

"But how free are you when you won't travel, you won't experience things outside your small world?"

"It's not small. I have all my people here. All the people I love. It feels huge."

"But what about Paris?"

She pulled a regretful face. "Maybe one day I'll get there."

"I'll make sure of it," he said, before he saw her face uplifted to his, her lips partly open.

"Kiss me," she said.

It would have been rude to refuse, he thought, as he pressed his lips to hers. From the first touch, he knew that this would be nothing like he imagined. It was like ice touching fire. The movement of her lips against his, her tongue teasing his, inhaling her breath, broke down the final barriers around his hardened heart.

Eventually he pulled away and they pressed their foreheads to each other's, breathing heavily.

"And there was me thinking you didn't fancy me sexually."

He lifted his head in surprise. "What?"

"I thought that perhaps you hadn't made an advance to me... you know, a sexual advance, because you were a gentleman and weren't like that."

He grinned, and did what he'd been wanting to do ever since he'd met her, he pushed his fingers through her glorious hair. "I *am* a gentleman but I like sex as much as the next man. No, I want to be honest with you. I like it possibly more than the next man. And I've thought of nothing else since I saw you in the street that first day when I was running."

"Hm," she moaned lightly, and the sound did things to his body which there was no way he was going to act on. She rolled on to her tiptoes ready to kiss him again. But he took her hands and stepped away with a shake of the head. He needed to sort his business affairs out first.

"I've got things to sort out, Amber, before we can take this any further." The doubt which flooded Amber's face nearly undid his resolve. "Amber, believe me. I really like you. I really do. But—"

His words were robbed by her mouth on his and a kiss which made him forget his name. Then she heard a rap on the door which was followed by a few more, before they eventually parted.

Amber shook her head as if she couldn't believe what had just happened and gave a shy smile. "I'd better get that."

Amber opened the door and the lady from next door stood there with a big grin, holding a large, angry-looking ginger cat. "Look who I've found!"

"I told you he wouldn't be far away."

David stood in the shadows, hoping that the neighbor would disappear. Amber too, he noted, hadn't opened the door very wide, but it seemed the neighbor had no intention of leaving. Instead she stepped confidently into the house, nodded at David, and sat down in a chair by the window which she obviously regarded as her personal space.

Before Amber could close the door, the neighbor on the other side greeted her heartily and, without waiting for an invitation, entered the room and greeted the woman seated with the cat. Neither seemed surprised to see the other. David couldn't help wondering if it was a set up.

The man and the woman began talking between themselves. Amber shrugged and smiled at David. David shook his head, bemused. No one ever entered his central city apartment without an invitation. In fact, he rarely gave invitations. He was a private person and, if he wanted to socialize, he much preferred to do it away from his own home.

The fact that people could treat Amber's home with such familiarity baffled him.

"Would you like a cup of tea?" Amber asked the couple. The man had now taken a seat in the opposite chair and they were talking about the museum. It seemed the man worked at the museum as a volunteer. More community stuff. They both nodded eagerly and David followed Amber through the bright plastic streamers which marked the entrance to the minute kitchen.

Amber plucked some brightly colored mismatching mugs from a stand and held one up to him. "Like one?"

He shook his head. "I'll get going. It looks like you're busy."

"It's strange, they always seem to pop round exactly a quarter of an hour after someone who they don't know comes to my house."

David didn't think it so strange. He suspected that Amber's neighbors, like her family and friends, would do anything to make sure nothing untoward happened to her. Knowing Amber's openness, there wouldn't be many people unaware of what had happened to her.

She put the kettle on a hob—David did a double take before shaking his head in disbelief—and turned to face him. "I've enjoyed this afternoon. Shame it couldn't have been longer."

"I've enjoyed it too." But David was grateful that the neighbors had stopped things from getting out of hand. It was too soon. He had things to remedy first. "Maybe... You'd like to come to dinner at my apartment next week?" He should be able to get things sorted by then.

She shook her head with a smile. "No thanks. I don't go to men's apartments."

He closed his eyes briefly at his stupidity. Of course she

wouldn't. "Dinner then. At a restaurant. Not St Augustine's. Somewhere more friendly."

She laughed. "That would be lovely."

"I'll check my diary and get back to you."

He reached out and drew his knuckles gently down her cheek. It was so soft. She instinctively turned and kissed his fingers. It was all he could do to withdraw. But withdraw he did, pushing his hands well into his pockets where they couldn't get him into trouble. He stepped away. "I'll call you."

"I'll look forward to it."

He walked back into the small lounge, unable to prevent a big grin on his face. The neighbors returned it. "You off now?" asked the man, jumping to his feet in an old-fashioned gesture.

"Yes. I've got to get back."

"Sorry to disturb you," said the old lady with an expression which showed that she wasn't in the least bit sorry.

"You didn't," replied David. "I was leaving anyway." He didn't want them to think he would in any way take advantage of Amber, although in a different way he had intended to. But no longer. "Goodbye."

Amber opened the door and stood there, casting a long shadow down the path as David walked to his car. "Goodbye," she called out. He waved back at her as she closed the door. He stood looking at the row of cottages for a moment. Amber's curtains weren't drawn and he could clearly see the three of them chatting and laughing in her front room. He stood, mesmerized by the view, before opening his car door and sliding in. Even then he dipped his head to get one last view of her—red hair flaming under the orange glow of the low-watt lamps, her clothes a flashing mix of colors as she flitted around passing cups to her guests before stopping in front of the window. She caught his gaze and, lifting her hand to him, wiggled her fingers. The simple gesture caught at his chest and plucked something there. He made an involuntary movement to his chest, beneath which he knew were his ribs and his lungs and another part of him which he'd only been interested in for its ability to keep him alive—to continue to pump blood and oxygen around his body. It seemed it had now acquired another function which was solely focused on this unusual woman who appeared like an angel in her window.

He waved back and turned on the engine, pulling his gaze determinedly away from her. What the hell was happening to him? He had no idea and, for once in his life, he didn't care. Because it felt right. He slipped the car into gear, gave Amber one last wave and drove the short distance to his sister's house. It seemed his world was suddenly growing a lot smaller, and he didn't mind at all.

6

The gray watery expanse of Lake Ellesmere slowly gave way to the suburbs of Christchurch, and still Amber leaned against the window of the car, fretting over her first exhibition at an inner city gallery.

"Aren't you excited?" asked Maddy, turning to Amber in the back seat of the car. "First proper exhibition and all that!"

"Yes, of course I am," she replied, still seeing the gray of the water in her mind's eye. It seemed to fit her mood.

"You don't look it."

Amber shrugged. Maddy was right, she didn't. And neither did she feel it. "It's just..." She sighed. "It's all happened so quickly."

"That's more reason to be excited. How David pulled it off, I don't know!"

Amber sucked her lip. Nor did she.

Gabe looked at her in the rear-view mirror. "Is the gallery owner a friend of his?"

Amber shrugged. "I guess."

"Don't you know?" he asked.

"No." She pulled her gaze from the growing suburbia and

looked at Gabe. "Want to know why?" She didn't pause for a response. "Because I've hardly spoken two words to him in the two weeks since I last saw him. And I thought we were getting on so well." She slumped back in the seat and rubbed her forehead.

"Over to you," murmured Gabe to Maddy. Amber couldn't even be bothered to glare at her brother. What was it with men and emotions? They came across all tough and yet didn't seem to be able to handle, let alone talk about, their feelings. If they had them. Amber grunted to herself. Especially David. He was the worst of the lot. Kissing her so tenderly and sexily one minute and then disappearing with hardly a word. What on earth could be so pressing that he made sure he didn't come anywhere near her for two weeks? But she knew the answer. Nothing. Nothing was so pressing. It was obvious that he didn't want to have a relationship with her. The kisses which she'd thought to be so wondrous obviously were significantly less wondrous for him. The exhibition? Well, she guessed that was either a friendly favor, or a parting thank you gift. Thank you for what, though? That was the question.

Maddy reached through to the rear seat, grabbed Amber's hand and squeezed it. "He's probably busy. Arranging an exhibition for you at a prestigious gallery is hardly the sign of someone not interested in you."

"I guess not. It's just…"

"What?"

She shrugged. "I don't know. How can I know what I don't know?"

Gabe's brow lowered in confusion.

Maddy squeezed her hand. "You can't. But he said he's coming, didn't he?"

Amber nodded.

"Then maybe you should ask him what it is you don't

know. Ask him why he's holding back, what makes him come on strong one minute, and then back off the next."

Gabe shot a quick smile at Maddy, obviously relieved that his beautiful wife was able to untangle Amber's thought processes.

"You're right, I will."

Gabe wasn't alone. Not for the first time Amber admired Maddy's mind—scientific, but with a good helping of empathy, which made her able to decode muddled thoughts with razor-like accuracy, and help Amber focus. And she had only one focus now, to ask David what the hell was going on.

"WHAT THE HELL'S GOING ON?" asked Angus, entering the open-plan office at the top of the modern building, flooded with bright winter light.

David looked up from the papers, which he and an engineer had been checking over. It wasn't the first time someone had asked him that very question in recent weeks, but then what did he expect when he put everything on hold for two weeks to do a major U-turn in his life?

"I think we're done here," he said to the engineer and then waited for him to leave the room, before he moved to the hard part of the U-turn.

"I've decided to keep the building." He indicated the black house opposite which, despite its look of Victorian solidity, was anything but safe and secure. "I'm going to upgrade it."

"What? Have you gone mad? I heard some rumors but thought my team had misunderstood. What's going on? What's changed?"

"I can't make it public yet. There are all sorts of hoops I have to jump through with the council and resource and building consents first. But I've set them in motion."

"And I repeat, what's changed?"

"Everything." He sat opposite Angus. "Everything," he repeated.

"What, are you in love or something?" Angus laughed at the stupidity of the notion. Then he looked at David's expression and his smile fell. "Jesus Christ, you are!" He jumped up and pushed his hair from his face. "I don't believe this! You, David Tremayne, don't have a soft bone in your body and yet you're intent on changing the whole course of our work together because you're in love? Who the hell is this paragon of virtue? Don't tell me you're back with Katherine again." He shook his head. "Anyway, it can't be her because there's no way she'd want that old place kept as it is."

David decided not to be drawn on the subject of love.

"It won't *be* as it is. It'll be renovated, renewed and improved."

"It'll cost a fortune."

David shrugged. "I have a fortune, so there's no problem, is there?"

"The problem is, David, that you'll be doing something you've never done before—you'll be wasting that fortune. If you carry on like this, you won't have any money left."

David knew that there was an outside chance Angus could be right, but there was a lightness to his spirit that made him not care. It was as if his whole world had shifted, giving him a different perspective on things. He'd literally changed direction and now all he could see was Amber—like a guiding light, pulling him towards her. And he knew that he was helpless to do anything other than surrender to that pull. Because it would bring him home.

"Can't stop and chat," he said with a grin to the bemused Angus. "I've an art exhibition to attend."

Before Angus could remonstrate, David scooped his phone off his desk and walked out the door.

~

AMBER LOOKED around the exhibition space with wonder, tinged with doubt. She could hardly believe it was her work hung with such care under the expensive lighting on the walls. But she felt ill-at-ease. There was something not quite right and she couldn't put her finger on it. David had managed to pull off something none of her family had been able to do and had got her an exhibition at the most exclusive inner-city gallery. So why did she feel so uncomfortable— like she was a gatecrasher and would be discovered at any moment?

Rachel followed her gaze. "This is amazing, Amber. Your work looks fabulous all grouped together like this."

"Hm," said Amber, "I guess." She turned to her sister. "You don't think it looks a bit odd in this setting?" She followed Rachel's gaze around the immaculate gallery. Its exterior wall was glazed to allow clear light in, controlled by electronic eaves which extended according to the time of day and season. It had been described to her as high-tech, but the word 'brutal' sprung to her mind as she surveyed the interior gray cement walls upon which her pieces were hung.

"The gallery certainly has a different vibe to your work, but in some ways it's kinda cool to have your bright paintings against such a stark background. It's almost as if your work is passing comment on the cold gray of the interior."

Rachel had lost Amber on the last point. "Yes, I guess," she said doubtfully. "Anyway, no one else wanted it. I've asked the café a couple of times, but they don't seem keen. They only want touristy pieces and my heart's not in them."

Rachel stroked Amber's arm in a loving gesture. "I should think not. They're too commercial for you. Your pieces are all about heart."

"Heart is all very well, but some money would be good too," she said plaintively.

Rachel turned her head suddenly as one of the gallery owners fixed a red dot beside a piece. "Looks like someone's just bought that piece." Amber turned with a squeal as they watched the owner move on to another piece with a red dot. Amber was too excited to squeal this time, Rachel did it for her instead. Soon they were following the owner around, watching as she placed a red dot on each and every piece.

Rachel gripped Amber's arms. "You've sold out!"

"She has, indeed," said the owner, coming up to them. "Congratulations! I'd be interested in seeing what else you have."

Amber listened to the gallery owner talk about the current state of the art market before losing interest and checking over her shoulder to see if David had arrived. Luckily Rachel was on top schmooze form, and did the talking. As soon as Amber saw the familiar tall, broad outline enter the room she made a beeline for him, weaving her way through the crowd of people, half of whom she didn't know. She wondered which of them had bought her work. She had no idea and didn't really care.

Forgetting her intention to stay cool until she'd had a heart-to-heart with David, she gave him a big hug. "My work has sold out!"

David grinned. "That's fabulous! What did I tell you?"

"The gallery owner has said she's keen for more of my work."

"Of course she is. This is the start of something big."

"Oh." Amber's smile faltered. "I don't know that I want anything big."

"Well," he said, "the start of something, anyway." He plucked two champagne goblets from the tray of a passing waiter and handed her one. "Here's to you, and success."

How could she not be swayed by David's version of success, with his seductive gaze captivating her? It wasn't until sometime later that she remembered her doubts. The stranger who made her remember hadn't bothered to return her polite smile. Instead, he'd turned a wry grin onto David as he pushed his way through to them.

"David!" said the stranger, clamping his hand onto David's shoulder. David swung around and didn't look overjoyed. "I'm surprised to see you here, with all this." The man waved his glass of champagne at Amber's artwork, spilling champagne on Rachel's dress. David interrupted him before he could finish his sentence.

"Angus. And I'm surprised to see you here. Looks like you're following me."

Angus positioned himself as part of the group, glancing around before his eyes rested on Rachel, who looked as voluptuous and glamorous as ever in a figure-hugging red dress, her dark hair in big curls framing her face and cleavage. Rachel didn't return Angus's smile as she flicked off the champagne which had landed on her breast. Angus's eyes dropped to her breasts and his smile widened.

Amber looked up to see Rachel's husband, Zane, scowling at Angus from across the room.

Angus stuck out his hand to Rachel. "I don't think we've met. I'm Angus, David's partner in crime." He didn't elaborate.

Rachel reluctantly extended her hand. "Rachel Black."

Despite Rachel's tugging of her hand, Angus kept hold of it. He frowned. "Haven't we met before somewhere? You look familiar."

"I host a cookery program. Maybe you've seen it."

"Oh yes!" Angus turned his back on Amber to get closer to Rachel. "Of course." But before he could say anything further, Zane appeared.

David's eyes creased into a small smile. "And I don't think you've met Rachel's husband before either, Angus. Zane Black."

Angus turned and had to lift his eyes in order to meet Zane's glowering look. "Ah," he said shakily. He immediately moved away.

"I thought you were meeting with some clients at three," said David.

"Yes, I said I'd be a little late."

"I think you should go." said David authoritatively. "They are important."

Angus moved away but shot David a dirty look. "Don't worry, I'll keep the business going while you have your change in direction. I don't know why you've come here to this weird little exhibition. Sort of thing you'd find in a junk shop, if you ask me."

Rachel gasped as Amber looked away with embarrassment, wishing the cold, gray concrete floor would open up and swallow her whole. But, even more distressingly, she felt he was right.

David shot Amber an anguished look, but it didn't make her feel any better. "No one did ask you, Angus," said David firmly, taking him by the arm and walking him away from Amber. Amber watched as David forcibly removed his partner from the exhibition.

"Who the hell was that idiot?" asked Zane, shifting from one foot to another, looking for all the world like he had when he played professional rugby with the All Blacks—as if he'd give anything to leap across the room and bring Angus down.

"Some friend of David's, I think," said Rachel, shifting closer to Amber. "Are you okay? He didn't mean anything by it, you know. He was just annoyed with David, I think."

"That's right," said David, suddenly appearing from

behind Amber. "He was just trying to get back at me because he was annoyed that he had to work. That's all it was." His eyes were fixed on Amber. "That's all. Besides, he wouldn't know a work of art from his elbow."

"So what are you doing with this idiot then, David?" asked Zane, still fuming quietly at both Angus's ogling of Rachel, and his insulting of Amber.

"You know?" said David, taking another couple of goblets of champagne and passing one to Amber. "I've been wondering that myself the past few days."

"I think I've seen him," said Amber suddenly, frowning. "Going in and out of the building opposite EarthFoods." She turned to Rachel. "You know, the building which the owners want to demolish."

All eyes turned to David. He shrugged, his face in a neutral expression. "Don't give Angus a further thought," said David. "This is your day, Amber, and you have a sell-out exhibition." He raised his glass and the others followed suit. "To Amber, may this be the first of many exhibitions. Christchurch today, Paris tomorrow."

Rachel grinned and they all clicked glasses. "To Paris!"

Amber forced a smile onto her face. They were doing their best to wipe the insult from her mind. But they couldn't entirely, for the doubt lingered. And so did something else. There was something nudging at the edges of her thoughts, something which made her uneasy. She couldn't quite place it, but she would.

IT WAS late by the time they left the exhibition.

"Let's grab dinner somewhere, shall we everyone?" asked the ever-sociable Rachel.

Luckily for David, it was Amber who declined. "I'm pretty tired, thanks Rach, I think I might head home."

"Would you like a lift?" David asked Amber.

She grinned up at him. "I thought you'd never ask." She turned to the others. "See you! And thanks for coming."

Rachel came over and tipsily pressed a lipsticked kiss on Amber's cheek, which she then tried to rub off. Zane laughed and put his arm around Rachel. "Come on, let's get something to eat."

Amber stood in front of David—her face flushed with success, one small glass of champagne and the early evening sunshine on her face—and David thought she'd never looked more beautiful. "How is it you seem to glow?"

She laughed. "Do I? Maybe that's why Mum and Dad called me Amber. Either that, or because I've got red hair."

"Or maybe it's because you've got lipstick on your cheek." He tried to brush it off with his thumb, but she caught his hand and turned his palm to her lips and kissed it. To his surprise, the kiss held no gentle feeling, but a passion which he'd only suspected lay behind that sweet exterior. It seemed the warmth Amber emanated came from a fire within. And he was scared he wouldn't be able to resist that fire.

"Come back to my place?" she asked, as she twisted around in his arms and put her hands around his neck. Of course his hands should rest around her waist. Where else?

"How can I resist you?" he murmured, as he brought his face a little closer to hers.

"I don't know. I'm hoping you can't."

"Maybe," he said, wondering if he could press his luck a little further, "I need a little more persuading."

She cocked her head to one side, her hair brushing his cheek. He nuzzled his nose into her hair. She smelled of lemons and fresh air. He thought he could stand there forever with his face in her hair. But she giggled and pulled away. "Your breath is tickling me," she said.

"I just want to go on smelling you," he said.

"That sounds weird."

"Not to me, it doesn't." He pulled himself together. "Now, shall we get back to Akaroa, if you've quite finished basking in your own glory?"

"Yes, I'd like that." He took her hand and they walked to the car. "You know, I feel so happy. Everything is going so well," she said with a big grin. "I've got my family. Dad's well and happy with his amateur dramatics, all my brothers and sisters have found their soul mates and put their troubles behind them. And I've just had the best thing that could ever happen to me happen." She glanced at David's face and burst out laughing, tapping him lightly on the chest. "You think I mean you?"

"Why should I think that?" he asked, with his best indignant face, utterly determined to refuse to admit that he had.

"Because you're a man," suggested Amber. "I was actually referring to the fact that I've finally had an exhibition." She turned around and walked backwards, her hand twisted across her body as she kept hold of his. She looked back at the art gallery. "And a swanky one at that. I still don't really know why they agreed to the exhibition." She glanced at him, and he looked away. "I mean, my work isn't their usual kind."

"Maybe they want variety," he said. "Anyway, the point is that they did, and it was an amazing success."

She turned around again and fell into step and squeezed his hand. "It was, wasn't it?"

It seemed like the moment for another kiss and David was, for once, very happy to follow his instincts. He'd meant it to be brief, but they ended up stopping and kissing for a few long moments, everything forgotten except each other. Eventually they parted to find people looking at them.

"Come on," said David, mortified to find himself behaving like a love-sick teenager. What the hell had got into him? "Let's get going."

Amber didn't seem to notice anything untoward. She beamed at the interested faces of passersby and carried on as if nothing had happened. But it *had* happened.

AMBER HAD MANAGED to capture his free hand as they drove back to Akaroa, and held it within hers, covering it and stroking it and planting little kisses on it. It should have made him feel silly, it should have made him run a mile, but it made him do none of these things. It brought out so many emotions within him that confused him. He didn't know so many existed. But he recognized the principal among them—love. And the power of it floored him.

He'd loved his mother, and he loved his sister and brother. He'd loved his pet dog, who'd died the night before he left home. He'd only been hanging on for that dog. But, for the rest, his life had been occupied with work and pleasure, the most important of which had been work. Anything else had been a passing distraction to allow him to return to work refreshed. He'd never, in his life, experienced anything like the depth of these feelings before.

"How are you feeling?" asked Amber.

He smiled at her perspicacity. "Fine," he said, and her face dropped a bit.

"Really? Just 'fine'?"

"Yes, I feel good."

"So, what have you been thinking about as we've been driving along—you've been very quiet?"

"I was thinking that I feel good." But even as he said it, he'd realized that he was lying. He'd been thinking a whole lot more. He never lied. "You're right. I was thinking that I really like you." Again, the words were a weak reflection of his thoughts. It seemed that years of practice had been effective—he couldn't describe his emotions even when he wanted to. He opened his mouth to speak but, instead, he shook his head.

She raised his hand to her lips and kissed it. "We'll be home soon and then you can show me how you feel."

David didn't think it could get better than that and put his foot on the accelerator.

As parking was limited in front of the cottages, David parked around the corner, close to where Gabe's doctor's surgery was.

Amber closed the door and glanced towards the surgery, where the lights were on. "Looks like Gabe and Maddy are home."

David slammed the car door, locked it and put his arm around Amber, hoping like hell she wouldn't suggest a visit. To his intense relief, she didn't. Instead, she rested her head against his chest and they walked down the hill.

Before them, the coast road ran along the beach front. The sky above the hills on the far side of the harbor was still shot with colors of the sunset. David didn't think he could remember seeing anything more beautiful. By contrast, the sea was dark and limpid, barely moving in the still evening. But it would be, he knew. The tide would be shifting under the perfectly calm surface. Nothing was ever as it seemed. He knew that. He also knew that the woman by his side was too trusting to know that. And it made what he'd done all the harder to think about. But he'd make it right. He'd already begun the process.

Without the car to herald their arrival, they managed to gain access to her house without alerting the neighbors. Amber only just managed to smother a giggle before she quietly inserted the key and they entered the house. She flicked on a light, then looked at him. "That's a sign to my lovely neighbors that I'm home. They insisted. They reckon they can't settle until they see the light."

"What if you're at Belendroit?"

"Then they can still see my light at Belendroit from over here. See?" She said, pointing to the distant promontory along the shoreline, its lanterns shining.

"But the lanterns are always on."

"Not that end one. It's dark now, and I always light it when I'm there. My neighbors know that, Gabe knows that. Everyone who knows me knows that." She turned to him. "And you know that now, too."

He put his arms around her and shook his head. "Everyone looks out for you."

"I know. It's nice, isn't it?"

"Yes." It was, but it still seemed strange to him.

He was about to kiss her, but she moved away and pulled the curtains a little. She looked at him with a shy smile. "There, a little privacy. Would you like a drink?"

There was only one thing he wanted, but he sensed she was feeling uncertain.

"Sure. A coffee would be great."

"I only have decaf, is that all right?"

He groaned inwardly. Of course she would. "Fine, thanks."

She grinned. "You and that 'fine' word. You know, I'm going to work on you, make you say something crazy and out there like 'great', or 'fantastic'!"

"And that's *fine* with me," he said with a grin. "My mind is going a bit crazy imagining what you might do to bring this great feat about."

Her smile faded a little. "I don't know myself," she said.

He sighed and looked away. It was all he could do to stop himself from following her like a little puppy dog, anxious for her petting, her affections. He pushed his fingers through his hair, suddenly annoyed with himself to be brought to such a low. What the hell was he doing?

"Milk?"

He turned with a smile. One look at her, standing, with strands of the plastic ribbons cascading over her shoulders and through her hair, and he knew. He was here because of her, and happy with whatever she could give him, because there was nothing else he could do. His feet wouldn't move away from her even if he wanted them to. And, right now, that was the last thing on his mind.

"Please." He took his coffee black, he suddenly remembered, as he watched her pour milk—was that soy milk?—into his coffee.

He went and sat on the cracked leather bucket seat covered with a crocheted throw. He fingered the felted bright blue of the throw and thought to himself that Amber was the only person he knew with a handmade crocheted throw. Not only possessing a piece, but covering an armchair with one. He suddenly had a flash of memory where his grandmother had been crocheting in a corner of their sitting room, beckoning to him as his parents rowed. He'd followed her into the kitchen where she'd closed the door, sat him down and made him a mug of hot chocolate. Was that his attraction to Amber? A feeling of relief from the stresses of life? A throwback to his grandmother?

But then Amber entered the room, lighting it up with her bright eyes and smile in a way that his beloved grandmother never had. No. His grandmother had been a practical, no-nonsense woman who'd instilled in him the values by which he'd lived his life. But she'd also been loving, and he'd felt safe with her. Grounded. And Amber certainly made him feel grounded—in touch with things around him. Connected. He groped for the word. Amber had reached into his heart, grabbed it and brought him back to life, connecting him with people and feelings and life. There was no going back now.

"Thank you," he said, accepting the dubious-looking cup

of coffee. He hadn't heard the purr or chug of a coffee machine coming from the kitchen, only the bubble of an old pot on the stove. He took a sip and was surprised at how nice it tasted. "Tastes good."

She took a seat beside him, tucking her legs under her. "Don't sound so surprised," she teased. "Just because I haven't got a thousand dollar machine. I found the old Italian condenser in a charity shop. It makes the best coffee."

He had to agree. He also wished she'd sit a bit closer. "It's good."

"Hm," she said, putting her half-finished cup onto the table. "This is nice, to use your favorite word. Being here with you."

"Yeah, it is."

"I bet it's a bit different to your usual Saturday night."

He shifted in his seat to face her, stretching out one hand along the back of the settee, and touched her hair, wrapping a curl around his finger. "And what do you imagine I usually do on a Saturday night?"

She shrugged. "Something super glamorous. Schmoozing with the rich and famous while women like Katherine laugh at whatever you say. The rooms would be decorated with expensive wallpaper covered with flowers and birds and bright colors. And light would be sparkling from chandeliers and the cut glass wine glasses and everything would be bright and lovely."

He thought of the modern industrial settings and apartments which were his usual haunts. "That's a pretty detailed picture you have there. But I have to correct you, I can't recall bright colors or light sparkling anywhere. In fact, most of my friends prefer a minimalist approach."

"Pop always accuses me of having too much imagination for my own good."

He was silent. In some ways she might, but in others she

didn't have enough. "And what about you?" he asked, determined to move the subject away from him which, given the circumstances, he found extremely uncomfortable. "What do you usually do on a Saturday?"

"Well, that depends. Sometimes I want to be here and potter about. Other times I hang out with my family at Belendroit. Then again, Gabe and Maddy go to the local pub a lot, so I join them. Then there's Rachel and Zane who live on Maori land. They have a huge whanau and I'm always welcome there. Then there's Flo at the backpackers. She's my best friend and…"

David had never considered he had a wide circle of friends, but he'd been content with those he had. But listening to Amber continue to talk about the people she hung out with made him feel like a Nigel No Friends. Eventually she finished talking.

"That's a lot of people." A lot of people who would disapprove of him. David wondered if there was any room in Amber's life for him. He also suddenly wondered if he was simply one of many. "Amber," he said quietly, moving his fingers from her hair to her cheek. He watched as he swept the back of his hand gently across her soft skin, before scooping back her hair and rubbing the back of her neck. Her eyes flickered with pleasure.

"Yes," she murmured from beneath closed eyes.

"Do you think there's room in your life for one very 'nice' man, who's pretty hopeless at showing his feelings?"

She opened her eyes and nodded. "Yes, I do."

He inhaled, leaned forward and searched her eyes, trying to figure out what he'd done to deserve this wonderful woman. "Good." He pressed his lips to hers. She sighed and shifted closer to him until he could easily put his arms around her, hold her face between his hands, as their lips moved sensuously over each other's. It was Amber who opened her mouth wider and touched the tip of his tongue with hers, triggering a lightning reflex inside of him.

One minute they were seated upright, the next somehow they were lying side by side, their bodies up close to each other's, seemingly not able to get enough of each other's kiss. When they eventually parted, Amber moaned and shifted her hips closer to his, brushing her lips against his. David didn't think he'd ever been so turned on. His fingers toyed with her strap. All it would take would be a slight flick to remove the straps from her top. It didn't look as if she was wearing a bra. And then his imagination ran wild as he imagined Amber, naked, in his arms. He shifted a strap and her hand went to his, holding it in place.

"I don't usually do this, you know," she said, in a still aroused voice. She cleared her throat. "I mean, I'm sure you think I'm pretty open about everything and I am about most things…" She trailed off.

"Just not about inviting men back to your house."

"Yes. I don't do that."

"Not ever?"

"Not since… that time. Everything changed after that."

"Ah, right." His imagination managed after a brief struggle to rein itself in again. "I don't want to do anything you don't want to do. You know that, don't you?"

She nodded. "Yes, I trust you."

He swallowed a flicker of unease. She could trust him now. Maybe not initially, but he'd made changes since then. "Good."

She went to kiss him again but the phone burst into song. She kissed him, laughing at the inappropriate tune, rolled off the settee, and picked up the phone.

It gave David a few minutes to take command of his body and sit up and knock back the remainder of his cold coffee, grimacing as he did so. But he needed something to take the edge off his arousal. As he stood up and walked around the small room, he noticed Amber become increasingly quieter on the phone. It was a short call and when she finished, she didn't turn around immediately. He came up behind her and leaned against the kitchen wall, flicking one of the colorful strands of plastic out of his face.

"Is everything okay?"

She turned around and gave a quick, uncertain smile, but her eyes looked devastated.

"What on earth is the matter, Amber?"

She blinked as if upset, but didn't answer.

"Who was that on the phone?"

"The exhibition organizer. She wanted to brief me on how the exhibition went." His heart sank a little. She wouldn't have, would she?

"And?"

She shrugged. "It went well, I guess."

He wished she'd look him in the eyes. He inclined his head to her, trying to see her expression, but her bowed head was in shadow.

He extended his finger and gently put it under her chin, lifting it so he could see her face. He almost wished he hadn't, because that wasn't the face of someone joyful—it was the face of someone who was hurt, and hurt by him.

She licked her lips to speak, but he knew what was coming. "And it went well because you arranged for most of the people to come."

He shrugged. "Well, I may have put out the word, but that's networking. That's just what you do."

"But they came for *you*, not for me."

"Does it matter?"

"Yes, David, it does, especially when there was only one buyer of all my work. *You*."

He bit his lip as her eyes filled with tears. She gulped as

117

she tried to hold them back. "You meant well, I know that. And it was... lovely, I guess. But I'd just hoped, you know, that more than one person had bought the pieces. That the pieces had been wanted for themselves, not because someone liked me enough to make a generous gesture."

"I'm sorry, Amber. I didn't mean..."

"You didn't mean me to find out, I'm sure."

"I bought them because I loved them. And I got in quick, if I hadn't have bought them so soon, others would have come in and snapped them up, I'm sure."

"Are you? Because I'm not."

"I'm sorry. I shouldn't have been so quick off the mark. I simply wanted this to go well for you."

"You're a nice man, David, and I appreciate it. I guess I'm just a bit disappointed with myself, with my work." She moved away, and looked at a piece, frowning. "I'll just have to try harder. Maybe you should leave now."

David nodded, his heart caught at the moment he realized that, instead of bolstering her confidence, he'd done the opposite. He'd made her *not* believe in herself.

"I'm so sorry, Amber. I didn't mean to hurt you."

"I know. It's just that I'd rather be alone now. I feel a bit down."

"Right." He nodded with a sigh. "Right." He picked up his phone and car keys, and opened the door. They exchanged 'good nights' politely, as if the kisses of only moments before hadn't happened.

And, as he walked back towards his car, under a sky from which all the colors of sunset had now faded, leaving only a blackness which seeped into his soul, he thought that he didn't know how the hell he'd ever make her believe in herself again. But he knew he wouldn't stop until he'd accomplished exactly that.

7

*S*unday was Amber's day off from the café, which was just as well as the mood which had descended on her last night hadn't lifted. She lay on her bed, pillows all around, gazing up at the mobiles which Aimee had made from shells found in Lantern Bay last time she visited. Trouble was, whenever she opened the window, a few more grains of sand found their way out from the spiral shells as they moved in the breeze.

But this morning her mind, for once, wasn't on the here and now, but on David. She felt foolish. She was used to her siblings treating her with affectionate dismissal, but not someone like David. She felt a connection with him, totally unlike any she had with past boyfriends. Rightly, or wrongly, she'd felt that somehow he'd seen through the superficial hippy exterior and seen her, the real her. The one that didn't need looking after, the one that was strong and independent and happy with her life. But it seemed she was wrong. By buying up all her artwork, he'd treated her just as one of her siblings would. Step in and take over to make sure Amber was happy.

She grunted with frustration, tossed off the bedclothes and put her feet on one of the many rag rugs which covered the bare floorboards which she'd painted pink. She liked pink. She looked up at the ceiling, and she liked purple. What was wrong with that? Why didn't anyone respect her, or take her seriously?

Grumpily she went and showered and dressed in one of her more outrageous outfits. She refused to let people influence her. And that was where she was strong, whether they knew it or not. If they underestimated her, that wasn't her problem, it was theirs.

AMBER FOUND Flo in the large garden, which was Flo's pride and joy. Flo was a real homemaker, and Amber appreciated the spirituality of it. She just wished she had Flo's practical sense.

"Flo!" Amber waved to her friend, who waved back and came towards her, peeling off her gardening gloves and dropping them onto the old table under the veranda she used for potting paraphernalia.

"Amber!" said Flo, giving her a big hug. "What are you doing here? I thought you'd got too busy to catch up with your old friends!" Flo grinned, but Amber didn't.

"Don't say that! I'm not like that, it's just that I've been…"

"Preoccupied?" offered Flo. "I'm not getting at you. It's been fun to see you get immersed with the Hot Green Eyes guy. How's that going, anyway?"

Unwanted tears sprang to Amber's eyes. "I don't want to talk about it."

Flo touched Amber's arm. "It's okay, we won't then. How about a cuppa?" She glanced at her watch. "Even better, how about a glass of wine? It looks like you could do with one."

"Oh," moaned Amber, her brows knitting as she tried to control her emotions, but didn't succeed. "I'd love a cup of tea."

While Flo went and filled the kettle over the Belfast sink, chipped from decades of hard usage, Amber slipped off her shoes and sat in the old-fashioned grandmother's winged armchair, tucking her feet under her. Flo shot her a warm smile. Flo once said that Amber was the sister she'd never had. But it was more than just that which connected them. Flo had been with Amber every step of the way since Amber's world had turned upside down five years earlier and knew far more than anyone else in her family about what had happened.

Flo plugged the kettle in, and leaning back against the sink, folded her arms. "It's been good, you know, seeing you happy again."

"I'm always happy!" said Amber, slightly scandalized that Flo could see through her.

"You're mostly happy," Flo corrected her. "But there's always a shadow lurking in your spirit. You've never been quite the same since—"

Amber held up her hand. "We vowed to never speak of it again."

"You vowed, I didn't," said Flo, pushing herself off the sink and opening a jar of home-made chocolate chip cookies. She shook some onto a plate and set it on the scrubbed pine table which dominated the old kitchen. She hooked a foot around a chair and dragged it noisily to the table and pushed the plate across the table. "Like a cookie?"

Amber normally loved Flo's baking, more than her own, she had to admit, but not today. "No, thanks, I'm not hungry."

Flo's eyebrows shot up. "You have got it bad!"

Amber knitted her eyebrows. "Got what bad?"

"Don't sulk, Amber, it doesn't suit you."

"Well, I don't like you suggesting that I'm in love… or something." She faded away, suddenly uncomfortable at the thought that she'd just admitted she was in love.

"I wasn't. But it looks like you are." She leaned forward and poured them both strong cups of gumboot tea. "That's good."

"No, it's not."

"Why not?"

"Because David is not the man I thought he was."

"And who did you think he was?"

"Someone… who was kind of perfect."

"Ah, now I see the problem. Perfection doesn't exist. You always were too idealistic. David is a man—a person even more prone to imperfections than women are."

Amber sighed. "I mean perfect for me." She jumped up and wandered over to the window, leaning against the frame as she took a sip of her tea. "Goodness knows I know perfection doesn't exist. I do really," she said in response to Flo's expression. "And I like people all the more because of it. But I thought David was different. I thought he respected me, but he thinks I'm as dumb and as foolish as everyone else does."

"No one thinks you're dumb and foolish, and I don't believe David thinks that either. Come on, Amber. *He'd* have to be dumb and foolish to believe that, and he's patently neither."

Amber gave a small grunt of disagreement. "Do you know what he did yesterday at my exhibition?"

Flo shook her head. "I had to leave early. But what could he have possibly done to upset you? It looked like it was a great success. I mean, all your paintings were sold, weren't they?"

"Yes, because he bought them all!" Amber crossed her arms and sat back, as if that explained everything.

"All of them?"

"Every single one."

"Well," said Flo, considering. "I think the matter is even more serious than I imagined."

"Exactly," said Amber, glad that she'd confided in her best friend.

"He's obviously head over heels in love with you, and will do anything to make you happy."

Amber did a double-take. "That is not how I see it."

"How do you see it?" asked Flo mildly, taking a sip of her tea.

"He tried to fool me, trick me, into believing the exhibition was a success."

"It was."

"You're as bad as him! I thought at least you'd be on my side."

Flo gave her a long look. "And what does Rachel think?"

"She doesn't know what I'm going on about. She thinks I'm making a mountain out of a molehill. But she would, because it's the sort of thing that she'd do, too."

"How awful. People wanting to make you happy. People who'd do anything for you."

"Flo! Don't you see?" said Amber, jumping up. "I don't need people to do anything for me. I'm not helpless."

"No one has said you are."

"I'm strong and independent, and I want to know that my art—which is important to me—has made it on its own, too."

"Do you really think artists have become successful on their own merit? Not through people they know? Come on, Amber, it's all about the people you know. Even amongst artists. Look at this place. It was falling down and I didn't have a penny to my name until Maddy came along and turned it into a destination for archaeologists and other university regulars, who just keep on coming. And that's led to investment interest."

"So, that contract you were signing the other day, it's going ahead?" Amber squealed, forgetting her own frustrations for the moment, as she realized what this would mean to Flo.

"Yes! Apparently no strings attached. Some sleeping investor with more money than sense. Again, one of Maddy's contacts. Or Gabe's… or someone's."

"You sound very vague."

"That's because I am. I don't know the name of the investor, only their agent and solicitor. But it's all above board. I'll be getting the money next month, to make improvements as I see fit."

"That's amazing." Amber jumped up and hugged Flo. "You can do all the things you've always wanted to do. You can get domestic help so that you can concentrate on the garden; you can get office help—"

"So I can concentrate on the garden! Yes! I know. It'll change my life!"

The door buzzed at the backpacker's end and Amber went to answer it.

"Leave it, it's okay, one of the guests will get it. They're all lolling around on the deck, anyway. It'll be for them, no doubt."

Then it went again. "Look, you get on with that"—Amber indicated the pots on the stove—"and I'll answer the door."

Amber was glad she'd come—her own frustrations had been forgotten under the influence of Flo's good news. She whistled as she half-skipped down the hallway and flung open the door. The figure standing before her was a little aloof, standing back, filling in the doorway with a dark shadow. But she knew that shadow. Under the close-cropped beard was the good looking brother she hadn't seen in five years.

"Rob?"

"Little sister. I didn't expect to see you here." With one large hand he hooked her towards him and gave her a bear hug. She'd forgotten how cuddly he was.

"Rob! I can't believe it's you! What on earth are you doing here? We thought you were coming next month. And what are you doing *here*, here, I mean?" She cast a look over her shoulder to see if Flo was anywhere near, but she wasn't. Amber closed the door behind her. "What are you doing on Flo's doorstep?" She didn't need to add that Flo was the woman he'd gone out with for years, before he'd broken her heart and left the country.

But it wasn't the same Rob who'd left New Zealand so long ago. This Rob not only looked taller and broader somehow, but there was something different in his eyes.

Amber could hear the footsteps approaching. It was Flo, coming ever closer.

"Thought I'd better come and find out what's keeping you," said Flo, just as she was about to round the corner. "Who—"

The words were snatched from Flo's mouth as if she were winded, as she set eyes on Rob.

Amber's heart sank. "It's Rob," she said, belatedly.

"I think she can see that," said Rob, stepping forward. "How are you, Flo?"

Flo was as white as a sheet. She moved her mouth to begin speaking, but nothing emerged. Then she shook her head, more definitely. She licked her lips as if to help her speak. "How am I?"

"Yes, it's been a while, and I want to know how you are."

"I'm…"

Amber held her breath, keeping her fingers crossed behind her back, hoping against hope that her dearest friend and her long-lost brother would make up, would put an end to the hostilities which had seen him depart for the other side of the world without a word. Not that Flo had written to Rob, either. Amber considered they were both as bad as each other.

"I'm busy," said Flo abruptly. And without saying a further word, she turned around and walked quickly out of the house. Rob's eyes followed Flo, lingering on the place he'd last seen her, when they both heard the back door slam.

"She's busy?" asked Rob, turning back to Amber.

Amber shrugged. "Flo is always busy. If she's not in the house, trying to keep on top of its maintenance, she's entertaining visitors, putting on music evenings—you know how much she loves music—or she's out in the garden. You know how much she loves the garden."

Rob gave a short nod. "Yeah." He'd barely smiled since she'd seen him. His mouth was a stern line and, not for the first time, Amber wondered what on earth had happened to him to turn him from a fun-loving youth to a stern, no-nonsense man. "I know how much she loves a lot of things, except me."

Amber looked up at her big brother, who she used to idolize, and couldn't believe he could be so stupid as to let someone like Flo slip through his fingers. "She used to, you know."

He closed his eyes briefly as if she'd taken a shot at him and had found her target. Apparently there was still a place of tenderness hidden away in the macho man who was her closest sibling. "No, I didn't know. She never said anything, despite…" He trailed off, apparently unable to say what he wanted to say to her. It made her heart ache. They'd used to be so close. He was always the first person she'd look for if she needed a cuddle, reassurance, or to know what to do. When Rob had left New Zealand out of the blue, it had hit the whole family hard, but it had devastated Amber. It had been shortly after that she'd accepted the lift from the boy she barely knew. Not that she could blame Rob for that. But that was a long time ago. She'd definitely changed and so maybe had Rob.

"You should go and see her," said Amber. "Have a chat."

"A chat? It didn't look much like she wanted to chat with me."

"Oh, I'm sure she does, it's just..." Amber drifted into silence. She couldn't think what to say without telling him the plain, unadulterated truth.

"Just?"

"Just that she's angry with you for what happened."

For a moment he looked as if he were about to say something, then he clamped his lips together into that firm line from which Amber knew nothing would be emerging. She didn't know what the hell had happened between Rob and Flo, only that their lives had gone very separate ways and left them both broken-hearted. And Amber's hopeful heart now hoped that they could resolve their differences.

He nodded, and looking decisive, followed Flo outside.

Amber watched her brother go. They were two good people, and she so hoped that they would get back together again. But she knew that Rob had a lot of groveling to do to make that happen.

Despite her curiosity, Amber didn't follow Rob outside. If ever there was a time to leave her friend alone, it was now.

And, she thought, casting around for her handbag, she had her own battles to fight. She checked her phone, which she'd turned to silent. She'd been persuaded by her family to have a cellphone, despite her innate distrust of them, and more often than not, had it on silent. There were unread messages from David and a number of missed calls. Well, he could wait. Battles, she thought, that might prove a whole lot bloodier than Flo's.

As she was leaving, she heard the landline ring again. She

wheeled her bike out of the garden and onto the road, remembering the first time she'd bumped into David there, and glanced toward the house where his sister lived part time. The blinds were down, presumably no one was home. She looked away suddenly. She'd promised her father she'd pick up some groceries.

Half-an-hour later Amber took a shortcut across the back lawn of Belendroit, ringing her bicycle bell madly. She waited for the expected barking and gamboling of the two cocker spaniels who ruled the house, but there was no sound.

She frowned as she leaned her bike against the tree and ran up the steps.

"Stanley! Boo! Pop!"

"I like how I come last in the pecking order," her father called out from the study.

She laughed and walked down the hallway, dropping the bag of groceries on the kelim-covered chair as she went. "It's because you don't usually bark when I ring the bell."

She stepped into the room and came to a dead standstill. There, at the desk her father only ever used to put things on, sat her father, glasses perched on the tip of his nose as he flicked through some papers. And standing with his back to the sunny French windows was the silhouette of a man, and not just any man. David. She'd recognize those broad shoulders anywhere. And, even more surprising, was that at his feet sat two cocker spaniels who both gazed at David, as if awaiting a command.

"David! I didn't see your car."

"I walked here."

"Walked?"

"Yes, walked."

"So, what are you doing here?"

"David's here on business, darling. He's getting involved in the museum trust."

"Museum trust?"

Jim Connelly signed his name with a flourish and pushed away the papers and sat back. "Why do you keep repeating yourself, Amber?"

Amber ignored the question and walked straight past David. "Coffee, Pop?"

Jim glanced from her to David and then back to Amber again. "Yes, please. Have you got my things?" He rose and looked into the bag. "Thanks. How much do I owe you?"

Amber waved an airy hand as she went into the kitchen, conscious of two pairs of eyes watching her. "Nothing. You never owe me anything."

"No wonder you never have any money," Jim said with a sigh. "I'll transfer it to your bank account."

Amber shrugged. "Thanks," she said vaguely. Money didn't concern her, something her bank manager was always nagging her about. She flicked on the tap and filled the kettle with cold water. She could hear a murmur of conversation between her dad and David, and she wondered what they could be talking about, and what kind of connection David had with the museum trust. They'd hardly hit it off the first or second times, so how come they were behaving like best mates now?

She flicked off the water and listened for a moment, but their voices fell silent. She began unpacking the shopping and putting it away, knowing that it was rude to ignore David but still feeling aggrieved by the fact he'd treated her like a kid to be humored, rather than an adult who could compete in the real world. He obviously thought she couldn't compete—not her, and certainly not her artwork. It was quiet in the other room, but still she lingered in the kitchen, waiting for the kettle to boil and then making some coffee. She got out some cups and turned around to place them on the table to find David silently watching her.

"You made me jump," she said, taking milk out of the fridge. "Do you normally stand watching people in silence?"

"Only when they won't talk to me. Besides, I was curious."

"About me?" She turned to face him, crossed her arms and leaned back against the work bench. "I'm surprised. I wouldn't have thought you'd think there was anything you didn't know about me."

He raised an eyebrow. "That sounds quite snarky, coming from you."

"Well." She turned away from him again and opened the cookie barrel, checking for non-stale cookies. "Then perhaps you don't know all there is to know about me."

"I never thought I did. What things do you think I should know?"

"That I'm not someone who needs help; that I'm an adult who should be treated like one; that, despite what it appears to my family and friends, I don't need cosseting. David, I know you meant well, but what you did shows me exactly what you think of me and my artwork—precisely nothing. You didn't think I stood a chance of selling anything in that exhibition, otherwise you wouldn't have stepped in and bought everything."

"That's not true, Amber. To be honest, I didn't give it much consideration, I simply wanted to–"

"Control me." She completed his sentence before he could.

"I don't wish to control you."

But even as he said it, she could see his frown deepen as he pondered the words which had fallen automatically from his lips.

"Are you sure?"

He opened his mouth to speak but grimaced instead. "I'm not usually in the habit of analyzing my actions to such a degree."

"Then perhaps you should start. I'm a free spirit and I don't wish, or need, to be controlled. And, unless you understand that, then I don't think there's any point you standing there gripping the wall as if you think you'll fall over."

"That's one of the things I love about you—your free spirit—why would I want to capture it?"

She shrugged. "I don't know. Hang on a minute, what did you just say?" She reflected on his words. "Did you say 'love about me'?"

"Yes. I love lots of things about you—your free spirit, your warm heart, your beauty, your kindness, your sweetness, your—"

She stepped toward him. "Go on," she said, more softly now.

He shook his head and his eyes never left hers. "I can't. I've forgotten. Whenever you come close to me, I forget what I'm going to say."

She stepped a bit closer. "David, I have a question."

"Anything."

"Why are you gripping the wall?"

"Because I'm terrified I'll walk right over to you, put my fingers through your hair, hold your face still and kiss you."

"Hm," she said, taking another step closer. "I'd like to see that."

"You would?"

She nodded. "I would."

"Does that mean you've forgiven me? Because, you know, I don't underestimate you, and I don't want to control you." He shrugged. "I guess it's just habit to jump on in, and take over, to seal the deal."

"You like sealing the deal, don't you?"

He loosened his grip on the wall and thrust his fingers through her hair, and brought his head close to hers. "I do. Preferably with a kiss."

She lifted her face to his. "Is that how you sealed the deal with Pop?" His lips were smiling as he pressed them to hers.

"So," he said breathlessly as they pulled apart. "Am I forgiven?"

"Yes. It probably seems silly to you, after all you did it to try to make me happy. But I'm not the kind of person who can be made happy by fake gestures. I really wanted to succeed, to share my art with people, not just one person."

"I get it. But promise me one thing."

"What's that?"

"Don't stop creating your art. Because it *is* beautiful and you just have to find the right audience." He hesitated as if he were about to say something else, but Amber knew what it was.

"And the audience at the gallery wasn't the right one, was it?"

"I don't think so."

"No. It should be somewhere where I hang out. The café would be perfect, but they only want touristy pieces."

"We—I mean, you'll find somewhere. I know you will. Look, I have to go."

"What could possibly be so important as to take you away from a sunny afternoon drinking coffee with me and my dad?"

"One word. Business. I have a lot going on at work. I'm making some big changes."

"Okay. So when will I see you again?"

"How about tonight?"

She grinned. "Sounds good."

AMBER LOOKED OUT HER WINDOW. Everything was gray and streaked with a misty rain. The sky and sea were a metallic gray while the hills on the far side of the harbor were a forest green, the individual trees combined into one forbidding mass. A silent sheet of lightning sparked behind the hills, somewhere out in the Pacific Ocean, flickered for a few moments and then was extinguished, leaving the gray even more opaque, as if it were being sucked into a darkness from which it couldn't escape.

Her skin prickled and she shivered. Something felt wrong, off, as if nature was trying to warn her. She gritted her teeth, determined not to be influenced by such things, forgetting that the last time she'd been so determined it had cost her dearly.

Whatever, it would rain. She hoped the road to Christchurch wouldn't be blocked by slips, which it often was after heavy rain. At least not until David got here. She grinned as the familiar low shape of his car revved as it passed her. She waved and it disappeared around the corner to park. She closed the curtains and opened the door, waiting for him to appear.

Despite the ominous darkness and threat of heavy rain, the air smelled good—alive, somehow. She stepped out into the drizzle just as David clicked open the wooden gate and strode up the garden path and into her arms. She literally fell into them and he took hold of her and kissed her as if he'd been thinking of nothing else except that kiss for a long time.

She curled her arms around his neck and he ended up carrying her inside. She pushed the door closed with her foot, only catching a glimpse of curtains twitching either side. She just hoped that what they'd seen would keep her neighbors in their own homes.

"Hello," she said, as they eventually parted and he set her down on her feet.

"Hello," he replied.

A sudden clap of thunder made them both turn to the

window which was illuminated as another bolt of lightning lit up the night sky, revealing a solid sheet of rain.

"You just missed the rain."

"It's been following me. I hope there's not a slip tonight or else I won't be able to get home."

"You could stay at your sister's, I guess," she said, with a smile, moving her fingers over his closely cropped hair, more evidence of his need for control. She hoped that she'd break that famous control tonight.

"No room," he said with an answering smile.

"Oh dear, then perhaps you should stay here with me."

"But the road might be clear."

"But you could stay here with me, anyway. I've plenty of room."

He looked around. "This looks pretty much like a one-bedroomed house."

"It is." She gripped his hand. "I'll take you to see it if you like?"

"I would like, as it happens."

She took him through a door in the lounge directly into the bedroom which sat parallel to the kitchen with the small bathroom added at the rear of the bedroom. Fairy lights twinkled around the wrought-iron bed—painted pink—and the multi-colored glass chandelier which looked as big as the small double bed over which it hung.

She opened the door wide. "So, what do you think?"

"It's exactly as I imagined."

She turned and nestled into him. She wanted to breathe him in, devour him.

"Well, it's not exactly as I imagined."

He looked down at her, lifting a stray curl from her face. "No? And how did you imagine this?"

She jerked her head to the bed. "You, me, on the bed."

He put his head back and laughed, before raking his

fingers through her hair and cradling her face. "There's never any pretense about you, is there?"

"No. Life's too short." A shadow came over her as she remembered. "For a long time, after..." She sucked in a breath to continue. "After what happened, I didn't trust anyone, not really. But you've changed that for me. I trust you, and I want to go to bed with you."

He blinked and froze. Suddenly, she couldn't read him. It was as if a wall had slammed down, concealing his thoughts, feelings—everything.

"David? What is it?"

"Amber, I'm not making love to you, as much as I'd like to."

"Why not?"

He was silent for a few minutes as he examined her face. "Because I don't think I've done anything to deserve that trust."

She was confused. "What do you mean?"

"Just that. Trust should be earned."

"You haven't *not* earned it," she said, groping to understand.

Again he was silent. "Amber, I love you. I really do. And, believe me, I never thought I'd say that to anyone. I think I loved you the moment I set eyes on you. I felt I could see you, the real you, so bright and hopeful and lovely, and I was drawn to you like a moth to a flame. But, frankly, I'm scared that I'll do something wrong. I want to take this slowly."

"Slowly," she repeated, grasping something she understood. "I happen to like slowly," she said with a spreading smile. "It gives time to savor and understand things better."

"And I don't want to misstep."

She took his hand. "You won't, because I won't let you," she said, pulling him to the bed.

There they kissed and lay down, and listened to the

increasingly heavy rain batter onto the iron roof above them, drowning out any other sound. And they got to know each other, slowly, and Amber realized it felt more intimate than sex, more loving than anything she'd experienced.

Later, they fell asleep in each other's arms, still partly dressed, but content and at peace, as the storm continued to rage all around them.

8

"*O*h my goodness, Flo, but David is the one for me! He's gorgeous and lovely and I'm in love!"

Flo picked up the last cup from the now empty veranda and stood holding a tray of breakfast things. "So you had a good night?" she asked dryly. But, it seemed, Amber wasn't in the mood for dry.

"Yes, yes, yes!"

"Three yesses, goodness. That was a good night!"

Amber followed Flo inside. Water still dripped from the holes in the rusting gutter, and the creek which flowed beside the house was high and noisy from last night's storm.

She closed the door behind her, darkening the hallway, the colored light from above the door bringing chunks of vivid color onto the polished floorboards.

"We didn't make love, though," Amber said, before greeting a couple of late-leaving backpackers in the hall who gazed at her with an open curiosity which Amber didn't notice.

Flo looked from the backpackers back to Amber with a

shake of her head. "Come on, we'd better go into the kitchen for this conversation."

Flo set the tray on the table and poured them both a coffee. "Now, about this making love business. What happened?"

"Nothing, honestly. Well, when I say nothing, we cuddled and stuff, but David didn't want to make love because he said he didn't think he'd earned my trust yet."

"Wow! He said that?" Flo grunted with admiration, before furrowing her brow. "Did that seem a bit strange? Why did he think he had to earn your trust? Has he done something to upset you?"

"No, of course not. What could he do? He's perfect!"

"Steady on. No one's perfect." Flo ruminated for a few moments. "Where is he now?"

"He's gone to work. Christchurch. Why?"

"I don't know. It's just that I've never heard of a man refusing to make love to a woman who's obviously keen when he's told her he loves her. It's just odd, isn't it?"

"No," denied Amber, doubt creeping into her mind for the first time. When she'd been with David, nothing had seemed odd. Whatever he'd said she'd believed and they'd been in tune, in key, together emotionally and spiritually, so there was no way she could doubt him. But now, in the cold light of day, she couldn't help agreeing with Flo. There was something odd about it. She stood up. "Anyhow, I'd better get going."

"I thought you were going to hang out with me this morning."

"Change of plan. I've had a text from a friend asking me for one of my rainbows on another building, which the powers that be want to destroy. And I think I'll catch up with David, too."

"Where? His office? His home?"

The seed of doubt grew a little. She didn't like to tell Flo that she didn't actually know where either of those were. All she knew about David was that he appeared from time to time in Akaroa, where his sister also lived part time. Really, it wasn't much to go on now she thought about it.

She shrugged. "Somewhere. I'll see him around." And, as she left Flo's place, she had the uncanny sense that she would.

But, at the end of a long, hot afternoon, Amber still hadn't seen David, despite sending him text messages asking if they could meet up. She stepped back from the painting on the side of the wall of one of the older buildings in Christchurch, now exposed by a building which had had to be demolished after the earthquake.

She'd been asked to join a group of artists who were frantically painting the front and sides of the lone building, which remained standing after the 2011 earthquake but whose future was far from certain. With empty lots on either side, it was ripe for development, and that was just what the group was afraid of.

She stepped away from her painting and scrutinized it. She liked it. Abstract, but with a feeling for the place. It might be ever so slightly illegal. But no one knew who owned the wasteland, and all the feedback on their work had been positive.

There were only a few of the group left that late in the afternoon, as it had got colder. She went and joined the others who were beginning to pack up. "It looks great, doesn't it?"

"Yeah. And your rainbow is perfect, brings together the two elements really well. You've got a way with colors."

Amber grinned. She might not get her work shown in

snobby art galleries in Christchurch without knowing the right people, but *her* people enjoyed her work. And that was good enough for her.

"It all works well together, doesn't it?"

"Yes, the news reporters who were here earlier took a few snaps and interviewed me. I hope it makes the news. We want as much publicity as this will bring us. It would be a crime to demolish it." Her friend waved one of his paint brushes across the road. "Look at those old warehouses. They've been done up and are tenanted now. So could this one be."

"Let's hope."

"Anyway, we're off now. You coming?"

Amber felt a momentary flicker of unease. She still didn't like being left alone, especially on a deserted site such as this. "Yes, I'll just pack my things."

But, as the others were itching to go, they made sure Amber wouldn't be far behind them, and hopped over the fence and were gone.

Amber finished up, gathered her things and was only a few minutes behind them, but they'd vanished and, instead, she was confronted with a small group of angry-looking men in suits.

"Hey!" An aggressive voice shot out over the cold frosty ground. The men were standing around the padlocked gate, which she'd hopped over a few hours before, watching her. She smiled and waved. Maybe they were sightseers doing the rounds of the art works.

"Hi!" she called, pulling her vintage purple coat more tightly around her. She wore a south American knitted hat with ear flaps, fingerless gloves and thick boots. Gabe had said she looked like a homeless woman when he'd caught sight of her. Maddy and Rachel had defended her look, saying no homeless women had ever looked so exotic, and besides, she wasn't carrying plastic bags. Amber didn't care either way. She never did understand why people worried about what other people might think. What was the point? No, she dressed to please no one but herself. And people had to accept her for who she was, or not at all.

"You there!" The voice was angry now, and her smile faded.

She put her brushes into her leather holdall and walked across to the fence. "Yes?" she said, through the wire fence.

"What are you doing there?"

She looked at the painting behind her and wondered why they were asking. It was pretty obvious. "Painting a rainbow."

A car door slammed from behind them. "Sorry I'm late. I got held up at the—" The words stopped like they'd flowed into a brick wall and Amber found herself face to face with David.

"We've found the culprit, sir. We'll let the police take care of this little matter."

Amber turned back to the speaker. "Culprit?" She frowned. "I'm an artist."

There was a snigger among the men and she turned back to David, her frown deepening.

"Tell them, David."

All eyes went to David. He, too, was frowning, as if unable to believe what he was seeing. He glanced at the rainbow and she followed his gaze.

"Of course, it's not finished yet," she said, embarrassed for the first time that she worked in such a rudimentary form, sketching, until something took off, and then working from that explosive center to the outside. For the first time in her life, she questioned her process. She wished she could begin in one corner and work steadily to the other, with no one ever doubting the quality of the artwork. But here, with others looking and the undercurrent of snide remarks and laughter, she suddenly felt embarrassed and hurt. She swallowed and looked up at him, wondering why he wasn't saying anything.

"Amber, I—"

"Do you know the woman, sir?"

"I do. This is Amber Connelly."

Amber waited for him to introduce them to her. But he didn't.

"And is she an artist?" one of the men asked him, as if she wasn't there.

"Does it look like that?" laughed another man.

She stepped back as if struck. "David?" she asked again.

David turned to the others. "Shut it!" he said to them, and they did.

"Miss Connelly, I must ask you to leave this area. It's private property," David said.

She couldn't believe he was talking to her as if she were a stranger. She opened her mouth to reply, but for the first time in a long time words proved elusive. She normally never had a problem speaking, because whatever was in her heart was in her mind, was in her mouth. But here, now, this man in whose arms she'd fallen asleep had turned into a stranger before her eyes.

"Miss Connelly?" she repeated in a whisper directed only at him.

His eyes, which she'd only ever seen to be strong and sure, reflected her own confusion. "I'm sorry, I…"

She stepped away again, shaking her head, unable to believe what she was seeing, what she was feeling. She licked her lips and bent down to pick up her bag.

"Don't forget your paint pots! Only the best in materials for the 'artist!'" shouted one of the men. She used exterior house paint rather than expensive oils. She had intended to make a second trip to return for them. But now she just wanted to get all her things and get away from the laughter, and this stranger who she'd thought she knew.

With her spare hand she balanced the cardboard tray carrying the pots of paint on her hip, and bit her lip as she looked at the gate over which she'd clambered only hours earlier. She stood for a moment, wondering how she was going to get out, not looking at any of them, trying to ignore the barely suppressed laughter and comments about her fledgling rainbow, when the lock in the gate clicked, and the gate was opened for her. David stood, his eyes fixed on hers, the gate open. The fact he'd opened the gate for her was a relief. The fact that he had the means to do that, held the key in his hand, confounded her.

She tried to lift her chin but was scared her watery eyes would be seen by everyone, so she kept her eyes down and tried to swallow past the lump in her throat, tried to clear the blurriness of the ground by blinking. It didn't work. "Thank you," she said in a clipped, proud way as she walked past him. She felt his hand on her arm.

"Wait, I want to apologize."

She bit her trembling lip. "Please take your hand off me."

For a moment she wondered if he would. But after a moment's hesitation, he did, and he stepped away, leaving the way clear. She walked along the street to the bus stop, knowing she'd missed the bus she'd intended to catch. It was too late for cafés, they had all closed down for the night, it being a week day in winter with few people around. Only crazy would-be artists, Amber thought miserably, allowing a tear to track down her heated face. Only artists of rubbish rainbows still lingered on the cold, darkening streets. She placed the tray of paint pots on the seat beside her and sat down on the damp wooden bench.

She could hear the drone of voices from the empty lot, punctuated by David's authoritative staccato instructions.

Whatever they were meeting about, it didn't last long and she soon heard the clank of the chains and lock being put into place. Why, she didn't know. All you had to do was climb over. But when she glanced over, she noticed that they'd added further precautions to the fence. A line of barbed wire. No one would be climbing over that in a hurry.

David looked at her and she turned away again, focusing on the incoming rain cloud sweeping over the rooftops. She'd get wet, she thought, numbly. The bus shelter was a work in progress and a roof had yet to be added.

She continued to focus on the gray cloud, the same color that had invaded her heart, she thought remotely, as she listened to the cars roar off down the road, leaving an emptiness which she felt to her core.

She swallowed hard, trying to push down the lump. But it was as if it were a cork which held tight her emotions, prevented them from emerging, and it stayed put. Just as well, she thought. There was enough rain now falling from the sky, tracking down her head and face without the addition of tears.

A car swam into her vision. Some top of the line gas guzzler, she thought reprovingly. It pulled up in front of her and a darkened window noiselessly lowered. A head dipped down and she saw those eyes. She knew they were green, but everything had become one color of gray in the gloom.

"Amber, get in."

She bridled at his tone. As if she were some stupid child who had to be told to get in the car. She wouldn't dignify his command with an answer. She looked away.

He sighed. "Please, Amber, get in."

If he thought using the word 'please' before a command would be persuasive, he had another think coming.

"For God's sake," he said, as the rain intensified on the roof of his car, and turned to hail. "You'll freeze out there."

At that moment a bus came along. "I'd rather freeze than sit with a rude man who I thought was my friend." She rose. "Anyway, here's a bus. Go back to your rich people to laugh about me and leave me alone."

He glanced in his rear vision mirror. "That bus is only going as far as Little River. You'll be stranded there."

"I don't care. I'd rather be stranded in the middle of nowhere than sit with you in that, that obscene thing you call a car."

His face creased. "Obscene? And I don't call it a car. I call it a Jaguar."

"You can call it a spacecraft for all I care." She held out her hand and indicated that the bus should stop. It stopped in a splash of water. She picked up her paints and ascended the steps. The bus was full and, shivering, she had to go to the rear of the bus and sit amongst kids, among whom was her niece, Etta. They quizzed her about the paint pots. She'd always liked kids, especially teenagers, and tried to focus on them, blocking David and his betrayal from her mind. She knew the pain would slam back with full force, but she had to get home first. Home to safety.

Etta glanced behind as they stopped at a bus stop. "Never been followed by a top of the line Jaguar before. Look at that!"

The others turned in their seats as the bus idled outside a lamp post which illuminated the car. She could plainly see David looking up at the bus. She looked forward again abruptly.

By the time they'd passed a few more stops, the teenagers were intrigued and making up stories as to why they were being followed. The passengers had thinned out by this time, leaving only them in the back seat.

"I think he may be following me," she said.

"Jeez! Is he some kind of creep?" asked Etta.

"I think he may be," Amber said, trying to keep cool and dignified, twisting her fingers in the rope of her bag.

"And he's waiting for you to get off so he can pounce on you!" Etta and the others were incensed. "He hadn't counted on us. We'll sort him out for you, Amber."

"That would be nice," she said, trying to stop her lips from trembling. She fixed her gaze on the dark window, but only saw herself reflected back.

They wound their way slowly over the hills towards Little River where they would have to wait for the last bus to take them to Akaroa. She didn't look again out the back window. She didn't need to. She saw the movement of the car's headlights illuminating the dark around her as they snaked their way to their destination. And she listened to the cat-calling and running commentary from the teenagers.

At last they stopped, and the bus rumbled as they jumped out. She went and sat in the bus stop—at least it had an overhead shelter to keep out the rain—while the teenagers went directly over to the Jaguar which had stopped behind the bus, and stayed there as the bus turned back for Christchurch.

Apparently oblivious to the threat of half-a-dozen teenagers shouting at him, David got out of the car and slammed it shut. He took one look at the teenagers, clicked it locked and went over to the bus shelter, closely followed by Etta and her friends.

"Amber. You are surely not going to sit here for two hours until the next bus, rather than take a lift with me."

She shot him a look she hoped could be described as filthy.

"Hey, perv!" shouted one of the teenagers, as they got bored with checking out his car and came up to him.

"Are those children talking to me?" David asked Amber.

She nodded. "Yes."

He sighed and turned around. "What?" he asked them.

"You, mate! You with your flash car. Just cos you're loaded doesn't mean you can stalk people, you know."

"I am not stalking anyone." He turned back to Amber. "What the hell are they talking about?"

"I suggest you ask them, not me." She looked determinedly away, studying a patch of graffiti scratched into the window of the bus shelter where there was a heart in which two names were inscribed. She hoped Shane and Jess, whoever they were, were prepared to be heartbroken.

"She's not talking to you. So why don't you just f-off and leave her alone?"

He turned to the teenagers again. "Because it's raining, she's missed the last bus—as have you all—and she's my friend."

They all looked back at Amber. How come it all sounded so rational coming from his lips?

"Is that right, Amber? Is this guy your friend?"

"Hang on a minute," said Etta. "I thought you looked familiar, you're that serious guy who came to Belendroit. Amber's friend."

He gave Etta a cursory nod before turning back to Amber.

"*Was*. Was my friend. Not anymore. Not since he was a bastard to me."

"Jeez, man," said another teenager. "How could you be mean to Amber?"

"You know Amber?" asked David.

David looked from the kids to Amber, then back to the kids.

"Yeah, of course. We watch out for each other round here. And you're not from round here, are you?" said one of the larger kids, stepping closer to David.

"No, no, I'm not. And you know? I'm glad you're looking out for her. But then so am I. Look, how about I give you all a lift back to Akaroa? I'll drop Amber off first, then the rest of you. How about that?"

There were nods of approval from a few of them, and within seconds three of them had returned to the car, and were peering in the windows, exclaiming at its luxury.

"Amber," said David. "Please, come on. I just want to see you home safe."

She licked her lips and shivers racked her body. "Well, I guess if they come with me it'll be all right. Because I have no intention of talking to you."

"You're talking to me now."

"Only a little."

He held out his hand, which she didn't take. She rose and walked over to the children. She could hear his leather-clad shoes clipping cleanly through the puddles, while her soft shoes were already soaked, and her feet freezing.

He unclicked the door and before he could say anything Amber had jumped in the rear seat with Etta and another girl, while the boy happily took the front seat, and immediately began touching the controls.

"Don't touch that," David said firmly. The boy agreed without comment as he stretched out in the car, one arm hooked over the back of the seat as he angled himself to the rear, while still running his fingers over the controls in the door.

"So, David," he said cheekily, "what do you want with Amber?"

Amber saw the muscle in David's cheek flicker, reflecting a struggle which she knew would be between telling the teenager exactly where he could go, and fitting in with them for her sake.

"To apologize," he said, his foot suddenly flat against the boards as he overtook a car. The kids whooped at the sudden speed and made gestures at the car they overtook, which Amber tried to stop. She didn't succeed.

"Go on, then," said Etta, from next to Amber.

Again, the flicker. "I'm sorry, Amber."

Amber continued to look stonily out the window, down which the rain wept as she wanted to.

Etta nudged Amber. Amber shot her a dirty look, which made Etta's eyes widen. "Aren't you going to accept?"

"You don't just accept apologies if they're given. It's not something you have to do automatically." She shot a black look to David's reflection in the rear-view mirror. His frown deepened.

"What did you do to upset Amber, David?" Etta glanced at Amber. "She seems pretty pissed with you."

"Yes, she is, and I understand why, and I'm sorry."

"But, David," said Etta, leaning forward so her head was closer to his in the front seat. Amber saw him try not to react. "The first question is"—she glanced at Amber with a secret grin—"what did you do?"

There was a pause in which none of the teens spoke. That, in itself, seemed a miracle.

"I wanted to destroy something Amber loved."

There were shocked mutterings. Amber's gaze remained fixed on the back of the seat in front of her as she tried not to cry.

"I reckon you two are pretty much stuffed then. You both want different things."

"No!" said David too quickly. "No," he repeated more softly. "It can't be like that."

"Why not?"

Amber waited for David's answer with curiosity, too. But it didn't come. His hands flexed around the steering wheel, but he didn't speak.

"Okay, so why, David, would you want to destroy something Amber loves?" asked Etta, showing the same kind of gutsy courage she displayed on the rugby field.

It seemed David was on more comfortable ground here. "Because it's a hazard. Because it would cost more to try to patch it up to earthquake standards than it would to build a new state-of-the-art earthquake-proof building."

"What's wrong with that, Aunty Amber?" asked Etta.

"Because those buildings are more than just bricks and mortars, they're our history and have the energies of the people who lived in them before. They're precious and should be preserved, not destroyed."

The boy in the front seat sniggered at the word "energies", but Amber ignored him. She was used to people not believing what she did. But, still, it didn't mean that her beliefs, and the buildings she believed in, should be destroyed.

"Well, David," said Etta, in the kind of 'let's sort this out' voice Amber could imagine her uncle and now step-father, Zane, using. "Even if you don't believe in the whole 'energies' thing, I guess it *is* our history."

Amber waited for David to refute it. "Yes, you're right. And Amber's right. I'd arranged to meet the others there today to tell them of my new plans." Everyone had their eyes glued to David.

"So why did you do this in the first place?"

"Because..." There was a long pause. "They're unsafe."

"And 'cos you're going to make a bomb, I bet!" said the boy.

"And because you want to keep people safe, eh, David?" prompted Etta, obviously trying to put the best spin on the situation as possible.

"Yes."

Nobody spoke as everyone waited for something more

from David, but nothing came. The silence continued as they entered Akaroa.

"Well," said Etta, eventually. "I guess keeping people safe and making a heap of money is good. Isn't it, Amber?"

"There are other ways of keeping people safe," said Amber. "Ways which cost money, rather than make it."

David's expression was grim as he pulled up outside her cottage.

"Thanks for the ride, mate. See you later, Amber!"

"Don't you want a lift home?" Amber shouted out in desperation.

"No. There's a party tonight just up the road from here," said Etta.

Amber got out of the car and, turning on the rain-slicked brick path, looked at David. He'd also got out of the car. She looked away.

"Amber, please don't go inside without letting me speak."

She paused, still with her back to him.

"You're right," he said. "I know you're right, now. You made me realize that I've gone too far. There's a place for both sorts of buildings."

A wave of relief washed over her. "Really?" She turned around to face him.

"Yes, really."

"So... what were you doing coming up to me today with those people?"

"I still have some business to wrap up. I was there to discuss with them the future of the project."

"And what is the future of the project?"

"To restore it."

She swallowed. "Are you just saying what I want you to say?"

He smiled. "And when have I ever done that?"

"True."

"I'm sorry, Amber. I'm so sorry that I misled you at the beginning. It's true, I thought I could get to know you and..."

He was at a loss for words, but Amber knew what he meant.

"And use me to get to my friends to stop what we were doing. People shouldn't use people."

"I know. I was wrong. Can you ever forgive me?"

"Honestly? I don't know. Can you be one person who destroys buildings and uses people one minute, and then change, becoming someone entirely different the next minute? I'm not sure that that's possible."

"I understand. But I don't think that person was the real me. *This* is the real me."

"So many yous. But how can I know which is the real one?"

"By letting me hang around, getting to know me better? Would that be okay?"

But, in that moment, Amber didn't trust her gut instinct anymore. And she really didn't know who the real David was. She shook her head.

"No. I don't think it would be okay."

David looked shocked, and she realized that he also didn't know her at all. She gave a sad smile. "I may look like a hippy pushover and I am to some extent, but I'm pretty tough, too. I know what I want, and I know what I don't want. Unlike you. I think you're the lost one."

The wind chimes around her front door clattered in the breeze.

"I made a mistake, and I'm sorry. But surely you're not going to throw away what we have because of that one mistake?"

"It was a big mistake, David, and it was mine. It was *me* who made the mistake."

"I don't understand."

"I told you once that I trusted a boy, I even told you what happened because of that trust."

His mouth tightened into a grim line.

"And," she continued, "you promised me that you'd never let anything like that happen to me again. You may not have raped me, David, but you deceived me, and took me for a fool. I'm no fool, and you're not the man I thought you were. You're not good enough for me, David." She nodded towards the car. "Now, please go."

He thrust his hands in his pockets and nodded. "I'm so sorry, Amber, for what I did to you. But I never meant to hurt you, and I definitely don't think you're a fool."

"I don't believe you."

"It's true. And I want you to know that I'm leaving now because of one thing."

Despite herself, she wanted to know. "And what's that?"

"Because I love you. I love you with all my heart and mind and soul, and I'm going to do everything in my power to make you love me, to earn that trust that you so willingly put in me at the very beginning. I'm going to show you, Amber, that we should be together and you will come to me again. I promise it."

She shook her head, which was reeling from his words. She opened her mouth to speak, but he raised his hand. "I'm going. And I won't return until you want me to. But I will do everything in my power to make you want me. Everything," he said, as he returned to his car.

Without watching him leave, she entered her house and closed the door. She leaned against it and closed her eyes. But it didn't stop the tears from tracking down her hot cheeks. She waited until she heard David get in the car and drive off before she brushed away the tears, turned on the light and filled the kettle.

This was her life, and it was a genuine one, one she

understood. And she refused to stray from it to a world where she didn't even know which version of a person was the real one. That way lay madness and vulnerability, and she refused to do that ever again. Even if it meant a broken heart.

DAVID WALKED to his car without a backward glance. He couldn't bear it—couldn't bear to think of what he'd done to Amber as anywhere near equating to what had happened to her in the past. And couldn't bear to think that she put him in the same category—someone who wanted her, only to use her. But hadn't that been the truth?

He'd prove to her that he loved her and could be trusted with her heart, that he'd do anything for her. But, as he roared off down the road towards his apartment in Christchurch, he wondered just how the hell he was going to do that.

9

*D*avid poured two coffees and joined his sister by the window which overlooked the waterfront and the tricolore—the French national flag—and stalls and kiddie rides that were set upon the usually empty reserve. He could see the sign for Amber's café and the occasional bob of a flame-haired woman who was constantly in his mind, whether he saw her or not. It was good to feel she was near.

Zoe turned to David and took a sip of her coffee. "Aren't you going to join in?"

"What?" David asked, knowing full well what his sister meant.

"The French Festival." She nodded to the scene outside the window. "Looks like fun."

Fun wasn't the word that sprung to his mind. It looked like heartache. "Have you been?"

Amber had disappeared, and he scanned the flapping canvas and bobbing heads before finding her again and relaxing.

"Yes," said Zoe. "I was there this morning. They even had a temporary path laid on the grass which I could navigate."

"That's good."

"Yes."

There was a pause as they both sipped their coffee, and David watched the bobbing red-head.

"Can you see her?"

David swung around to face his sister. "Who?"

"Who do you think? Amber, of course."

"What makes you think I'm looking for her?"

"Just a wild guess." She sighed. "Come on, David. You've got to cut yourself some slack."

Something crumpled in him then and he said down opposite Zoe, his back to the lively scene outside the window. "How can I? I stuffed up."

Zoe wheeled her chair closer, so it bumped against his knees, and stared at him. She huffed a sigh of frustration. "For as long as I can remember, you were always there for me. And since Mum and Dad died, you've played an even bigger part in my life. But, you're right, you've stuffed up here, big time. But you're not the man I think you are if you don't do something about it."

David rubbed his eyes. "I'm trying. I'm re-working my business."

"I'm not talking about business. I'm talking about Amber. You said you loved her and, if that's correct, you need to do whatever you have to, to make things right between you."

"But I don't know what to do. If she doesn't want to see me, I can't make her."

"Maybe not. But you'll have to do to yourself, what it is you're doing to your business. You'll have to show her you've changed. *If* you have." She sat back. The challenge issued.

He jumped up. "Of course I have. She's changed the way I see everything."

"Good heavens! My powerful brother changed by love. I never thought I'd see the day."

"You're not the only one," he grumbled. "What am I going to do, Zoe?"

"You're going to go over to that park, see Amber, and tell her you're not giving up on her. And you want to know why?"

"Why?"

"Because I'm not giving up on *you*. You can do this, David. You can let down that guard on your heart which you so successfully erected when Mum died, and you can let love into your life." She reached out her hand, which he gripped. "It won't hurt, I promise."

"How can you know that?"

"Because we're talking about Amber, here. And, from what you've told me, what I've heard about her, and what I've seen just this morning, she's not going to take your love and throw it in your face."

He looked out the window at the festival which was now beginning to pack up for the day. Could he do it? He felt as if everything sure in his life was falling away, and he didn't know what would be left after it had fallen. But there was only one way to find out.

He stood up.

"Are you coming with me?"

Zoe smiled a big smile of relief. "No, I reckon you need to do this alone."

He paused at the door and turned to her. "Tell me, Zoe, truthfully. I didn't get all of this"—he indicated the home he'd built for her in place of the old cottage which had stood on the site for over a century—"wrong, did I? I only wanted to stop tragedy happening to other people. I can't bear to think I was so wrong."

"You weren't. You've done lots of things right. You've saved lots of people's lives. It's just you've gone a bit too far now. It's time for a change. Time to think of yourself, time to be less black and white about things."

He grunted in amusement. "Time to put color back in my life. Time to have Amber in my life."

"I think so. Good luck."

As he kissed Zoe goodbye, left her house and crossed the road, heading toward the park, he thought he'd need it.

"AMBER, COME AND JOIN US!" called Rachel, who was capably juggling a small baby, a glass of wine, and refereeing between their brother, Rob, and their father, Jim. It looked like all her family had turned up and were now crowded around a table set up beside Amber's café's stall.

"In a minute. I just need to tidy up."

Amber sighed and went back to cleaning the trestle tables and packing the remaining food and quirky chinaware back into the baskets.

Akaroa's French Festival was drawing to a close, but the sun still shone, unseasonably warm. All Amber wanted to do was to go home and be alone. Her mind and heart were full of David's betrayal. She couldn't think of anything else.

But it looked like she wasn't going to get her way.

Rachel sent Rob off to find Flo—why, Amber didn't know, because Flo had gone out of her way to avoid Rob—deposited her baby on Zane's lap, and came over and began stacking the plates into a box for Amber.

"You don't have to do that," said Amber.

"No," said Rachel, emptying out some half-glasses of water onto the trampled grass. "I don't, but unless I do, you'll never sit down with us."

Amber shrugged but didn't reply, just kept on wiping the now non-existent crumbs from the table top. Truth was she didn't want to sit down, she didn't want to stop because then she'd have to think and thinking hurt—both her brain and her heart.

Suddenly Rachel's hand pressed on hers. "Stop, Amber. You're done here." Rachel tilted her head so Amber had no choice but to face her. "Okay?"

Amber nodded and looked away, tossing down the cloth and wiping her hands on her apron. "Okay." She squinted into the sunlight. It was the last day of the festival and it wound up mid afternoon, so the sun was still high. "Okay," she repeated, looking around to see what else there was to do. There *was* nothing. Rachel had finished tidying things up. All that was needed now was to take the boxes to the car.

"Say it once more and I might believe you."

Amber turned to Rachel but didn't say it the third time. There was no point, she wouldn't be fooling anyone. She'd lost her heart, had it trampled on, and now felt broken. She wasn't sure she'd be mending any time soon.

"You go back to everyone. I'll just finish up here."

Rachel shook her head, her lips pursed, but she agreed. "I'll get Zane to help you lug the heavy stuff to the car. And then, Amber"—she took hold of her arm—"come and join us and have a big glass of wine."

"I'm not in the mood for drinking. Or talking, come to that."

"This is *so* not like you," said Rachel. "You have to try to get over it."

"Do I? Maybe I'll just live with it, see how that goes." She realized her tone sounded bitter, and she never sounded bitter. Rachel looked even more worried, and Amber took pity on her. She sighed. "Don't worry about me. I'll be fine." She kissed Rachel on the cheek. "You go back to your baby." They both turned to see him being jiggled on Zane's lap, his arms reaching out to Rachel as he uttered an insistent squawk.

Rachel smiled. "Okay, but join us, yes? I can't bear you looking so sad."

Amber nodded and watched Rachel walk away and be swallowed up by the Connelly and extended families. She turned quickly. She didn't want to see them, or be a part of them today. The sooner she was done, the quicker she'd be home.

She bent down to pick up a heavy pallet, but another pair of hands beat her to it, and she looked up into green, green eyes.

"David!" She jumped back, her hand pressed to her chest where her heart threatened to jump from. "You made me jump."

"Sorry," he said, standing up, his hands full. "Are these going in there?" He indicated the open boot.

"Yes, but…"

He didn't wait to hear what she was about to say, and all she could do was collect some things and follow him to the car. He loaded them carefully into the boot and Amber was briefly distracted by the sight of his muscled arms as they pushed the heavy load into the car. Then he stood back, his hands on his hips, and looked around. "Is there anything else you need shifting?" He looked at her straight, as if their last conversation hadn't been life changing and emotionally charged. All she could do was shake her head in disbelief.

"No?" He checked around. "Then what about those?"

She glanced at where he was pointing. "Yes, sure. I need to take those back to the café, too."

"Then why did you shake your head?"

"Because I can't believe you're here, helping me, after how we left it."

He nodded and looked down, continued to nod as if wrestling with what he was about to say next. Then he looked up, fixed her with that intense green stare which still made her go mushy inside, whether she wanted it to or not. "Amber, I'd like to talk to you. Can I visit you some time?"

"I don't believe we have anything to talk about."

"But there's something I want to say."

She folded her arms. "Say it then."

He looked around. "Not here. Somewhere in private."

She grunted. "No way. You think you can get me on your own and persuade me you're not a bastard?"

"No, I don't want to persuade you about anything, I just want to talk."

"The answer is no. Now, if you'll excuse me, I have to go." She tossed the last tablecloth into her bag and walked over to her family. She cast one last glance at David, who was striding over the grassy reserve where people were busy dismantling tents and tables, where children ran and teenagers gathered, heads together, laughing, as older people looked on and reminisced. It felt like the whole world was there, but Amber's eyes watched only David, taller than the others, his step purposeful. He might believe he'd changed, but he looked no different to her. He still looked like a god, made of different stuff to the rest of them.

"Hey," said Maddy. "What's up?"

Amber turned to Maddy and forced a smile. "Nothing."

Maddy frowned. Amber's smile obviously wasn't very convincing. "Doesn't look like nothing." Amber glanced towards where David was last seen, and Maddy followed her gaze. "Was that David?"

Amber nodded and allowed her smile to fall. It was all she could do not to cry.

"Oh, Amber." Maddy gave Amber a hug. "It'll be all right. I'm sure of it. Look how Gabe and I were. I thought it was all over, but then it came right in the end. And I'm sure it'll be the same for you and David."

"Are you? I'm not. We're opposites. He's everything I don't want, and yet he's everything I do want."

"Oh, that sounds confusing."

"Yes, it is."

"So, what's he doing here, anyway?"

"He wanted to talk to me. But I don't want to talk to him."

"Talking might be good?" Maddy suggested tentatively.

"No. Talking would be bad."

Maddy followed Amber's gaze to where they could see David getting into his car and driving off at an uncharacteristically slow speed in the opposite direction to Christchurch. "That's a shame."

Amber sighed in agreement.

"Come on," said Maddy, putting her arm around Amber. "Let's go join the family."

"No, you go," said Amber. "I'm going home. Tell them I'm feeling tired, will you?"

"Sure."

And, for once, her family didn't follow her, but let her get into her car and drive the short distance to her home. She knew they could see her from there. See her from across the reserve to her row of cottages. She knew they could watch as she parked her yellow VW—she'd offload the stuff the next day—and walk up her path, greet her neighbors, and open her door. But she knew they wouldn't be able to see her tears as she closed her door.

She automatically went to the kitchen, filled the kettle and placed it on the hob to boil. She leaned against the kitchen bench and looked out through her small rooms, to the sunny reserve in the distance, her mind full of one question—what was it that David wanted to say to her?

. . .

162

AMBER HAD THOUGHT she'd managed to escape interfering family and friends, but when a knock came at her door, just as dusk was falling, she realized she'd been mistaken. Couldn't they take a hint?

"Yes?" she said briskly, opening the door wide, prepared to tell her family where to go. But instead, her gaze lowered to a woman in a wheelchair.

"Oh, hello!" said Amber, with an uncertain smile.

The woman had long dark hair and was beautifully made up. She looked familiar somehow. She smiled back. She could have been a model, if… Amber's gaze flickered down to the wheelchair. It looked custom built, it looked permanent.

"Hello, Amber."

Amber's smile widened as she racked her brain trying to think who this beautiful woman was. She gave up.

"I'm sorry, but if we've met before, I've forgotten. Brain like a sieve."

"We haven't met. We have a mutual friend who's told me a lot about you. And I've seen you around. I recently moved here."

"Oh," said Amber, wondering whether she should invite this stranger in. She didn't look as if she'd do Amber any harm. Her brothers were always warning her not to invite waifs and strays home. "Would you like to come in for a cuppa? The kettle's just boiled."

"That's lovely of you, but I'm not sure you'll want me in your house once you know why I'm here."

Amber laughed. "I doubt that. I can't imagine you could do anything except light up a room you're in. You're so beautiful!"

"You're exactly as he described."

A warning tremor zapped through Amber. The smile faded, and she frowned. "He?"

"Yes. He said you were sweet as sweet could be. I said you couldn't be. But he insisted. Seems he was right." She extended her hand to Amber, who had no choice but to take it. "I'm Zoe Tremayne, David's sister. And I'd like a few minutes of your time to tell you why you should give him a second chance."

Amber was rarely speechless but, as she stood there on her doorstep with her mouth wide open, not a word of response came into her brain. Of course she knew David had a sister, but not one who was both beautiful and in a wheelchair. And that this unknown sister should choose to pay her a visit with the intention of pleading his case astounded her.

"A second chance?" she asked, echoing the words because she wasn't able to summon up any original ones of her own.

"I do understand that my idiot brother doesn't deserve a second chance. What he did was unforgivable but"—his sister scrunched up her lovely face in what could only be described as an adorable, charming manner—"I love him and would do anything to make him happy."

"I understand that. I'm the same with my brothers, but…" Amber shrugged. How could she tell this woman that there was nothing she could say that would make Amber change her mind? That David had been the rat of the highest order, and nothing Zoe could ever say would change that?

"Please, Amber? Just a few minutes?"

Amber never had been good at standing her ground. She sighed and gestured helplessly with her hands. "Okay, but you'd better come in."

"Thank you! I appreciate it."

Amber squeezed around the chair and tilted it up—it was surprisingly light—to raise it over the threshold and into the narrow hall. "They didn't make these old cottages with wheelchairs in mind," said Amber.

"At least your cottage has an excuse—it must be over a

hundred years old. The same can't be said for more recent buildings which I can't get into."

"That must be frustrating," said Amber, wheeling her into the lounge. From there Zoe took control and spun the chair around, rucking up one of the rugs a little.

"What a lovely place you have here." She shone that hundred-watt smile on Amber once more. "David's description didn't do it justice."

Amber felt her own smile fade. Had David told his sister absolutely everything about her? Her own discomfort at the thought must have shown. Either that or what Zoe lacked in physical ability, she more than made up for in empathy and understanding.

"David doesn't tell me everything. It's just that"—she grimaced a little—"I don't get out much and so I ask him a lot of questions."

"Why don't you get out much? You seem pretty mobile."

"My decision. After my accident, I became a bit reclusive. It wasn't the life I had imagined for myself, you see. A million miles from what I wanted. It's only recently that I've emerged from that pit of despair."

Amber perched on the edge of her seat and wrung her hands in sympathy. "It must have been awful. What happened?"

"The Christchurch earthquake is what happened."

"Oh no! Were you trapped?"

Zoe nodded. "Yep. I shouldn't even have been there. I should have been in London doing a fashion shoot for Burberry, but at the last minute they'd postponed a few days and I shot home to see some friends. Then one of them called and left a message for David to give him a lift. But David wasn't there, so I went instead. Our friend worked on the top floor of a hundred-year-old building." Zoe looked into the mid-distance, lost in her memories. "Charming, totally charming." Then she re-focused on Amber. "A totally charming deathtrap, as it turned out. Our friend died that day under the rubble. And for a while I wished it had been me. It was selfish. Stupid of me, I know. But there it is. I couldn't see a future without the use of my legs."

"But you do now?"

"Yes. And there's only one reason for that. David. He's been everything to me these past few years. He's kept me company to hell and back and made sure that I *did* come back. But it's affected him too, and that's what I wanted to come here to tell you, because there's no way on this earth that he's ever going to stick up for himself and tell you."

"Why not?"

"Because he's too damned proud. He wanted to use you, Amber, to help him get rid of the opposition to demolish that old building you loved so much. But he wanted to use you for one reason only. And that was because he'd vowed never to let anything like what happened to me, happen to anyone else. He sees it as his personal mission to make sure that there's not a building in all of Christchurch which would collapse like a pack of cards like the one I was in did. And I suspect there's an element of guilt involved, too."

Tears sprang to Amber's eyes. Damn him. David was using her to make sure everyone else was safe. Damn him. She shook her head. "He used me, Zoe. From the first moment I saw him, while I was believing all sorts of other things, which he let me do, he was scheming to use our... friendship, for his own purposes. How can I ever trust him again?"

"He did a stupid thing, Amber. There's no getting around that. It was mean, and it was stupid, but he did it for all the right reasons. He did it to prevent anyone else from getting hurt. Now, I'm pretty sure there are all sorts of ethical dilemmas and reasoning which would both speak for and against David as being a good or bad man." She shrugged. "But I'm no academic, no theologian. All I know is that he's a *good* man, and he did something stupid in the act of trying to do something good, and he now regrets it with all his heart."

The heart which she'd accused him of not having, Amber thought. "I don't understand why he didn't tell me this."

"Maybe because he doesn't think it should excuse him. Maybe that now he reflects upon what he's done, he agrees with you. He doesn't think he's good enough for you. Yes, he did tell me that that's what you told him. He's placed you high on a pedestal and doesn't believe you can do any wrong, and he equally doesn't believe you should be with anyone as flawed as he is. But he's my brother, and I know him inside and out, and, while he might be flawed, he's a good man, with a kind heart. He'd do anything for the people he loves. Anything. And I'm just hoping that you might find it in your heart to see him again."

"You want me to forgive him."

"I didn't say that. Just see him again. He's so upset about what's happened. Look, there's much more to his story, and mine, than I've told you, so if you ever want to hear more, give me a call. In the meantime, please, just see him?"

Amber moved her head, but it didn't form a straight nod or a no. And it obviously didn't convey a straight answer to Zoe either, who shrugged.

"Well, I've said my piece and it's over to you. I'll leave you now."

Amber felt shell-shocked and simply nodded. She followed Zoe as she carefully maneuvered the wheelchair out of the room. As Amber opened the door and helped her over the threshold, Zoe stopped on the path.

"You have an amazing view here, right around the water to those lights in the distance."

Zoe's gaze lingered on the lights of Belendroit, almost

wistfully. Amber stepped forward beside Zoe. She pointed to the distant promontory with its two chimneys peeping out from behind the high trees. "That's Belendroit. One of the original homesteads."

"Oh, that's the place! I've always thought it looked pretty special. Very mysterious. And at night… those lanterns! I can see them from my house."

"It *is* special. Mum continued an old family tradition. She died when I was twelve." She turned to Zoe with a bright smile, forcing away the sad memories. "Like her mother before her, my mum insisted that lanterns always be lit for her children, to light their way home." She blinked. "I never like to be far away from them. If you're ever lonely, you'll know a Connelly isn't far away. In fact, you should pay Pop a visit. He loves meeting new people."

Zoe's face brightened. "I'd love that. I know so few people in Akaroa."

"Well, you know me now, and I'm just around the corner, and you know Pop. Or you will do."

"Thank you. You're very kind." Zoe extended her hand to Amber. "Thanks for letting me say my piece, Amber. I appreciate it. Whatever you decide over David, I hope we can catch up some time."

Amber shook Zoe's hand and then impulsively bent down and kissed her cheek. "That would be nice," Amber said, speaking, as usual, from the heart and not giving herself time to think it through.

But, after watching Zoe approach the taxi and the driver help her into the car, she closed her door and couldn't help wondering whether it would be nice, or acutely painful. Because there was no doubt about it, Zoe was a mirror image of her handsome brother. And, if she couldn't have David, would she want a constant reminder of a love that had gone wrong before it had had a chance to begin?

10

*D*avid approached Belendroit with trepidation. He'd arranged to meet Rob there but had got held up in Christchurch. He walked up to the quiet façade of the beautiful building, its lanterns clearly visible on the vines which were only just beginning to bud, and knocked on the door.

He could hear a radio being turned off and feet stomping up the hallway. His heart sank. It had to be Jim. The door swung open and Jim stood there, his face dark with anger.

"You've a damn cheek turning up here!"

So, Amber had told him. Of course she had. She didn't have secrets, unlike him.

"Is Rob here?" David asked Jim, dispensing with the usual formalities.

Jim looked grim and, for the first time, not in the least intimidated by David.

"No, he's not. I believe he said he had business with Flo." Jim stepped outside. "You're not welcome here, David. You tried to use our Amber for one of your business schemes.

That's despicable. Leave here and don't come back. You're not welcome. And don't try to see my daughter ever again."

With that, Jim slammed the door closed on David's face. David blinked at the colored paned glass which still rattled in its frame. He'd had doors slammed on him before. He didn't get to be so rich or powerful without garnering some bad feeling, but he'd never felt so small in all his life.

"Right," he said to himself, turning away and looking at the rutted driveway, bereft of Amber's rundown car. "Right," he said, looking up to the steep hills which surrounded Lantern Bay. The mist had already descended on it, blocking out any late sunshine, shrouding the whole place with a mournful light which David couldn't help think was wholly appropriate. It was as if someone had turned off his own light, leaving him floundering, rudderless, like the pontoon out at sea where the family would swim to. Except he wasn't moored. And, without that anchor, for the first time in his life, he felt he could easily slip away, taken by the current out to the sea, to be lost in its mad confusion.

It was a strange feeling. He'd lived a rigidly controlled life for so long that he didn't know if he could live any other. But he had to try, because he had to face his fears, exactly as Amber had had to do. Different fears, but they could be conquered in the same way, by not allowing them to run his life. It was as if the fulcrum upon which his life was balanced had changed—it was no longer fixed into an uncompromising position, unyielding to any influence, but was a basis of what was right. At fourteen years of age, the only right he had known was routine and control. But he was older now, and he could rely on a different guide. He knew what was right now.

FLO HEARD the knock on the door. He was here again. She knew it without having to see him. Rob. The man from her past, the man who'd broken her heart years before and seemed intent on not letting her forget it. She'd even kept a low profile at the French Festival the previous day in order to avoid him. But it seemed Rob wasn't about to let her.

She busied herself emptying the dishwasher, even as she was aware of the shouts of greeting from the backpackers who were staying at her hostel. Her place was an open house. She listened to the footsteps coming toward her, ringing on the bare floorboards of the hallway. He was a tall, broad man with a steady step which quickened the tempo of her heart.

"Flo," greeted Rob.

Flo stood up, sighed, and turned around. "Rob," she said. "What is it you want?"

"I want to help."

"I don't need your help, so you can leave."

"You're getting it, anyway."

"What part of 'I don't need your help' don't you understand?"

"The part which ignores the fact that you most definitely *do* need help and money. Look around you."

She didn't look around.

"I might need help and money, but not *your* help and money."

He grunted. "Well, sorry to say, but that's what you got." His phone buzzed. He pressed the screen, barked in a command and looked out the window. "Good, he's arrived."

"Who has? What's going on?"

Rob walked to the window and waved. He turned to Flo. "It's David. I'm bringing him in to help advise us on some of the construction issues."

"What the hell?"

"Haven't you understood by now? Flo, you always used to be so quick."

She eyed him dangerously. Much more of that and she'd put into use the right hook which she'd once used on him.

He ignored her warning scowl and took a further step toward her, and her heart beat a little faster. It had nothing to do with anger.

"Flo, you signed the partnership papers the other day, right?"

She nodded. "How do you know?"

"Because I, Flo, am your new partner."

He didn't wait to see her response, which was just as well, as she wasn't sure if she'd scream, thump him or burst into tears. Instead, he went to the front door which rarely got used, and opened it for David.

"Morning, Rob. Flo," greeted David. "An interesting place you've got here," he said, looking around. "It's great you've kept it untouched all these years. We'll be able to keep all this after ripping it apart and strengthening it."

"*Ripping*?" She looked from one to the other of them. "No one, and I repeat, no one, will be doing any ripping. In fact" —she strode over and pushed them toward the door—"you can both leave right now."

She reached around them, opened the door and pushed them out. "*And*, gentleman, don't bother coming back."

David looked from the door to Rob. "What's going on? I thought you'd bought into the business with Flo?"

Rob shrugged. "Yeah, I have. I just forgot to tell her. I couldn't quite figure out how to, so I reckoned I'd let it take its course. Must say that I didn't imagine it going like that. But Flo always was on the fiery side."

David grunted. "Well, as we've got some time on our hands, do you fancy going out to Christchurch and looking at some property there?"

"Sure. But I heard all that was underway."

"Change of plan."

"Nothing to do with a certain woman who happens to be my sister, is it?" asked Rob with a grin.

"Might be," said David. He didn't grin.

Rob looked puzzled and shook his head. "But—"

"I know, don't ask," said David.

Rob cocked his head to one side and shook his head again.

"Don't," warned David.

Rob took a deep breath as they walked to their cars.

"I'm sorry, David, but I don't understand."

"Look, I'll level with you. You know my business, it's always been about knocking down damaged houses and putting good, solid modern buildings in their place."

"The opposite to me." Rob grinned.

"Yeah, well, I'm changing my business model. That's why I wanted to work with you."

Rob grunted approvingly. "You *have* changed. So the building Amber's cooperative rents from you—EarthFoods— that's not going to be demolished now?"

"That's right. My structural engineers are working on plans right now to upgrade and reinforce. To do whatever they have to do to make the building safe."

Rob raised his eyebrows in surprise. "That *is* a change in direction. This will rock the Christchurch building scene bigger than the earthquake."

"I intend it to. I want everyone to know about the changes I'm making."

"And all this is because of our Amber?"

Our Amber? Rob's sense of family possession over Amber jarred. She wasn't their Amber, she was *his*. Or, at least, she would be his, because he couldn't imagine life without her. She *had* to be his. And so he would show her that he'd reinvented himself; he'd show her that she could trust him, he'd earn that trust. He'd become the man she'd first fallen for.

∾

"AMBER!" Jim Connelly said, jumping up from the veranda where he'd been reading the paper in the warm afternoon sun. "What are you doing here? Shouldn't you be at work?"

Amber ran up the last steps from the beach and petted Stanley and Boo, who'd been sleeping at Jim's feet and hadn't heard her approach. So much for being the guard dogs which Jim claimed them to be.

"I took a day off work."

Jim's glasses slipped down his nose as he looked over them in surprise. "You did what?"

Amber sat down and Boo jumped onto her lap and settled down for a good cuddle. "I took a day off work. Mental health day."

"What's wrong with your mental health?"

"Nothing. Well, nothing much. It's just a thing you can do these days for sick leave. You know, you don't have to be dying to take sick leave. If you feel stressed or burned out, you can take sick leave."

"Why are you feeling stressed? What's happened?" His eyes narrowed as he sat down. "Is this about a boy?"

"If you call David a boy, then yes it is."

"I doubt even David's mother called him a boy."

"You happen to be right there. I've just come back from visiting a new friend, Zoe."

"Who's that? I haven't heard of her before."

"Zoe is David's sister. And she was telling me that David has had to be a man since his mid teens because of what happened to their parents. To cut a long story short, after David's mother died, their father lost the plot, and it was left to David to raise Zoe and their younger brother, Adam. You're right, he hasn't been allowed to be a boy since he was fourteen."

"Good heavens!"

"I know. Tough, eh?" Amber felt the tears that she'd shed when Zoe had told her what had happened to their family, prick her eyes again. Zoe had told her how David had made sure they were kept together as a family and that Zoe and Adam had everything they needed to gain a good education and career, despite their father's fall into alcoholism and subsequent disappearance. David had run the household like clockwork, everything regimented, everything controlled, because he'd had to. David had been scared to let anything slip, Zoe had explained. And that need for control had only been compounded by Zoe's accident.

Jim pulled off his glasses and rubbed suspiciously watery eyes. "That explains a lot."

Amber didn't answer but, instead, rubbed Boo's tummy as Boo lay, blissful, on her back, legs splayed in the air. "Yes." She gently moved Boo onto the sofa and rose. "It might go some way to explaining why he wanted to use me to stop opposition to the demolition of the EarthFoods building."

"He underestimated you."

"Exactly. He thought I was some hippy pushover, to be wooed and used."

Jim wriggled on his chair, obviously angry at the thought. "If I see that man anywhere near here again, I'll—"

"You'll what?" interrupted Amber. "Make a scene? There's no point, because I've told him I'm not interested in someone I can't trust. And there's also no point because I understand he's moving to Akaroa, so you'll be seeing him a lot, I should imagine. As will I, whether I want to or not."

"He's what? What the hell does he want to move here for?"

Amber shrugged. "Who knows? Anyway, I'm not here to talk about him."

"Oh?"

"Yes, I wanted to run something by you. You know the money you've kept in trust for me. I wondered if you'd release it."

"Why? What for? You're not thinking of going away, doing something silly, are you, because of this David mess?"

"It's not a 'David mess', and no, I'm actually thinking of doing something quite serious. I want to buy the café."

"*Your* café."

"Yes, *my* café. In a way it *is* a response to David. After what happened five years ago, I think I've been running scared. Making all my decisions based on fear."

"Oh, darling," Jim said, putting his arm around her. "We've all tried to protect you, to keep you safe, that's all."

"I know, and I love you for it. But in the long run, it's not helping me. I want to do something for myself now, and it took David to make me see that. For all that he wanted to use me, he ended up making me believe in myself, making me think I could take control of my life. And that's exactly what I want to do. I want to buy the café, use it for exhibitions of my own, and other things I'm interested in. It's the right venue for it. There's enough touristy places already in Akaroa, and my work isn't right for upmarket Christchurch venues. No, the café is perfect. I know the owners have been considering selling for some time and they'd be keen for me to take over."

"Goodness. I can see that it would make sense. But running the café, Amber, the business side would be quite…" He trailed off, obviously unsure how to express the fact that he had no faith in Amber's business acumen.

Amber smiled. "I know. I'd be hopeless at the business

side, that's why I thought of Maddy. She'd be the perfect partner."

"Madeleine!" Jim nodded. "That could work. Is she interested?"

"I haven't spoken to her yet. I wanted to check with you first to see if you think it's a good idea and if the money is available."

He looked at her with a smile. "I do. I think it's a great idea. Perfect, in fact." He grunted a laugh. "All my girls following in their mum's footsteps—chefs."

It was Amber's turn to laugh. "Not me, Pop, you know that. I'll leave the cooking to someone who can do it well. I'll be there to hang out with people, make it into my kind of place."

"And that, darling, is exactly what Akaroa needs. Your kind of place. It's perfect."

And, as Amber left to track down Maddy, she thought it might not be perfect—because how could it be when she felt as if there were a hole in her heart—but it would be the next best thing. A project and a future which she could make her own, depending on no one, being controlled by no one. Hers alone.

It was raining by the time David reached Amber's house. He parked the car in the carpark down the road, there being no parks close to Amber's cottage. Despite the increasing heaviness of the rain, David walked with his head up, his gaze fixed on Amber's cottage, trying to discern signs of life. Unlike the other cottages in the row, Amber's, snug in the middle of the row, was dark.

He stood on the pavement beside which the sea had crept in over the sands and now lapped meekly at the stone wall alongside which the coast road ran. Behind Amber's cottage, the hill rose steeply to a row of grander houses above. Wasn't she in? Maybe she'd gone to bed already? But a quick check at his watch revealed, despite the gray skies and strengthening rain and misty atmosphere, it wasn't yet seven.

All the lights were on in all the other cottages. It made the absence of light even more stark. He could stay there all night, he suddenly realized, getting more soaked by the minute in his thin shirt—it hadn't been raining when he'd left Christchurch—but nothing would change. He was scared —scared of what he'd find in Amber's house. He'd avoided emotion for so long that it seemed it scared him more than anything. The thought made him angry and spurred him on.

He clicked the latch on the small cross-barred gate and walked up the short path. The drooping flowers and lavender brushed past his legs, releasing their perfumes, and the wind chimes which hung from the gnarled branches of the pohutukawa tree tinkled in the wind. He glanced through the window and was relieved to see the flicker of a candle. Of course, Amber wouldn't sit in the flooded artificial light of an electric bulb. She was a candle kind of girl. He liked that about her.

He was about to knock on the door when it opened. Her hair was rimmed with the soft golden light of the candle, which flickered in the hallway behind her. She looked like an angel. Then she stepped closer to him.

"What do you want?"

Make that an avenging angel.

"I'd like to apologize."

She gripped the door in a most un-Amber like way. "Apologize? And you think that would make everything all right? You think I'd accept it, jump into your arms and allow you to carry me to bed? Is that right?"

He hadn't, but her description led his mind astray and he

was speechless for a few moments. Moments in which she stepped closer and prodded his chest with her finger, her eyes glittering as amber as her name. From the angel, she'd just transformed to devil. Somehow he liked that just as much.

"No. Not at all. Well, only if that's okay." He winced as soon as he'd spoken the words. It was true. If she'd make it easy for him then he was more than happy to grab the easy option.

She lowered her head and narrowed her eyes. He could have sworn sparks emerged from her eyes. But it must only have been the way the candles flared in the draft from the door, reflecting light in her eyes and casting doubt in his soul.

"Please, Amber. Could you spare me a few moments? Let me speak and then I'll leave. I promise I won't darken your door again if you don't want me to. But I couldn't leave it as it was. Okay?" He tried to give her his best smile, but he suspected his lips hadn't moved if her reaction was anything to go by. "Please, can I come in?"

"No. I'll hear whatever you have to say here, and then you can leave."

He had to admire her. He'd angered women in the past, but none had stood up to him quite so strongly. Any resistance had always been overcome when he'd fixed an expensive necklace around their neck, or handed them first-class tickets to the Seychelles. Some he'd just had to kiss. He'd been spoiled, that much was obvious. But it stopped here and now, because there was no way Amber was going to let him off easy, if at all. That much was clear.

"I'm an idiot, Amber. An absolute idiot."

"Well, at least that's one thing we agree on."

The rain had begun to seep under his thin jacket and trickle down his neck, but he knew he couldn't leave until

Amber had given him some sign that everything was okay between them. He had no choice but to go back to the beginning.

"It's true that I first came to the café because I wanted to get to know you."

"To *use* me, you mean."

He grunted and gave a short nod. He couldn't quite bring himself to agree to that, even if it were true. "To get to know you. I'd seen your rainbows, and they were causing me no end of headaches, and I wanted to see the person behind them."

"So you could put a stop to it."

"I could have got the police to do that. You were painting on my property."

"But you knew that we'd continue, because it wasn't just the painting, it was that we were right—"

"Yes—"

"And that you were wrong. And you won't admit it."

"I just did," he said quietly. "You and your friends were right all along. I was wrong, and I'm sorry."

Her eyes widened and lost their glitter. "You are?"

"Yes. I shouldn't have been so rigid, so dogmatic as to impair my judgement. I was wrong, Amber. Wrong in so many ways. Wrong about the building, I should have listened to you and to everyone else, and wrong in my dealings with you. I'd always prized honesty, and yet I somehow lost the plot when it came to you. And I know why. Because I was scared I'd lose you. I'd always intended to have a rational talk to you, make you see sense and then leave it at that. What I hadn't planned was on falling in love with you."

Something like a whimper escaped Amber's lips.

"I love you, Amber. And I want to marry you. That's why I came."

Another whimper, louder than before. "Okay. Perhaps you'd better come in then."

She opened the door and stood to one side to let him enter. He stepped into the wooden-floored hallway, leaving a puddle around his feet.

"In fact, I think you'd better come into the bathroom. I'll get you some towels."

He followed her through the living room and sat on the side of the old-fashioned claw-footed bath. He gave his hair and face a cursory wipe.

Amber leaned against the side of the door, watching him. He hadn't a clue what she was thinking. She hadn't said anything since he'd proposed, apart from hand him some towels.

"Are you hungry?" she asked.

It was a better offer than nothing. "Yes."

"Shame, because I haven't got any food you like." His heart plummeted again. "I have some home-made hummus and vege sticks." He felt as if he'd suddenly been transported back in time to when his mother had gone through her vegetarian phase. Thankfully, it hadn't lasted long.

"That would be…" He was about to say lovely but didn't want to say anything he didn't mean.

"Nothing like what you want." She finished his sentence. "Well, come and sit by the fire, anyway."

He followed her into the small sitting room where flames from a log fire flickered along with the candles. The pretty large-flowered wallpaper which, he knew, was usually used only for a feature wall against some stark floor-to-ceiling window or brick wall, was here on all four walls. As he sat in the proffered bean bag and sank down, his wet trousers uncomfortable, he felt as if he were in some kind of nest of fire, flame and flowers. It was a strange feeling. Perhaps he was coming down with a chill. He closed his eyes without knowing it, but her soft voice broke through.

"So, what is it you want?"

"First, to thank you for allowing me in. I know I don't deserve it."

"That's down to your sister."

"Zoe?"

"Yes, she came around yesterday and I went to see her this morning. She filled me in on you."

It was a strange, disorienting thought that Zoe and Amber had been talking about him behind his back.

"It's the only reason I've let you in," Amber continued.

He could guess what Zoe had told Amber. "My family history is no excuse for what I did to you. And I've come here tonight for one reason only." He stood up, relieved from the discomfort of being squashed in a bean bag in damp trousers.

She rose, too, meeting his gaze with a steadiness and strength which unnerved him. He realized exactly how much he'd underestimated this woman. "And what's that?"

"To tell you that I've changed. That I've moved my business practice here and intend to run it from Akaroa."

"I know. Your sister told me." She folded her arms. "What I don't know is why."

"Isn't that obvious? Because you're here. And wherever you are, I must be close."

"But I've told you I don't want you."

"And I respect that. Don't worry, I won't stalk you. I won't even come near you from now on unless you invite me to. But I want you to see me around, and know that it's not only words, but I'm putting my words into practice. I'm changing, Amber, and that's down to you."

"Well, good for you, David. But it's nothing to do with me. We don't have a relationship anymore, if ever we did."

It struck at the heart of him. He hadn't known it would be

this painful to allow himself to feel again. But he also knew how precious this feeling was and that he'd never turn back.

He nodded. "Of course. Whatever you want. But, please, can we be friends at least?"

She didn't say anything immediately, and it was as if his life hung in the balance. Then she nodded. "Okay. Friends." She stuck out her hand, and he took it, full of intense relief.

"Thank you."

Too quickly, she slid her hand from his and opened the door. Before he knew it, he was back out in the wet street.

"Goodnight, then," he said.

"Goodnight," she said quietly, before closing the door.

But, as he walked back to his car, he remembered the look in her eye as she'd closed the door. That bright anger had gone, replaced by a warmth in which he found hope. It was enough for him to cling to for now.

11

"Glad to see you back in the land of the living," said Maddy, looking up from her laptop and plucking one of Gabe's invoices from the antiquated spike on which he placed them.

"I only took one day off work," said Amber, automatically turning on the coffee maker which Maddy had introduced into Gabe's otherwise basic kitchen. She hooked her bag on the back of a spindle-backed chair and sat down opposite Maddy. She looked at the cool beauty and, not for the first time, wished she possessed a tiny bit of Maddy's composure. Even if she knew that, beneath it, Maddy was every bit as emotional as the rest of them.

It was four in the afternoon and the early spring light was beginning to shift to a rich glow which shone through the front door and down the wooden-floored hall. If Belendroit was Amber's second home, then Gabe and Maddy's place—which doubled as Gabe's surgery—was her third home. Ever since the day Maddy had arrived in Akaroa with only a backpack and a secret, they'd been fast friends.

The coffee machine light shone steadily and Amber rose

and made three cups of coffee. Gabe's surgery would be finishing soon and there was no one in the waiting room which she'd passed. She brought two cups to the table and glanced over Maddy's shoulder at the spreadsheet, which looked incomprehensible to her. She placed a cup of coffee beside Maddy and took her seat once more.

"It's amazing how you can use spreadsheets."

Maddy looked up with a smile in her eyes. "No more amazing than how you create your art." She glanced back down at the screen and rapidly typed some entries. "Lucky that we're all types of amazing."

"Yes, it is," said Amber, cradling her coffee.

Maddy snapped closed the laptop. "But I guess you didn't come around to talk about spreadsheets."

"Actually, I did."

Maddy opened her eyes wide and reached for her coffee. "Really?"

"Yes, really. I have a proposition for you."

"And what's that?"

"Well, you know you said that you planned to reduce your hours working for the university, now you're pregnant."

"Yes," said Maddy slowly, obviously wondering where Amber was going.

"Well, I wondered if you'd be interested in a business venture. Working from home, around the baby." She nodded to Maddy's pregnant stomach.

"What kind of business venture?"

Amber licked her lips. Ever since the blow up with David, she'd been thinking about her life and what she wanted. It had all become clearer when she knew what she *didn't* want. She *didn't* want to be reliant on anyone else for her future. She *didn't* want to be dependent on a man for her emotional or physical needs, and she *certainly* didn't want to go cap in hand to an art gallery to only have them look down at her work.

"I don't think the owner will take much persuading to sell the café. I want to buy it and I can run it easily enough, dealing with the food and the people, but I can't run the business side and wondered if you'd come in with me as a partner."

The words had tumbled out, and Amber held her breath as she waited for Maddy to answer. Her hands tightened around the coffee cup but she didn't drink from it, because she couldn't be sure she wouldn't splutter. As soon as the idea had entered her head, after David's comment about the café being a reflection of her personality, the notion had refused to leave.

"What's brought this on?" asked Maddy.

Amber hadn't expected Maddy to reply directly immediately. It wasn't Maddy's way. But she was still a bit disappointed.

"David." She took a sip of her coffee and pushed it back onto the scrubbed pine table. "Something he said about how people went to the café because of me."

"That's true."

Amber shrugged. "I don't know. But it made me think. David had arranged the exhibition for me because I hadn't managed it myself. But I should have tried harder. I shouldn't have let him take control. It wasn't his fault, it was mine. And I intend to rectify that. For all the mistakes David made, he did actually make me feel more confident and make me think bigger." She sat forward in her chair, eager now. "You see, I thought I could use it to show my work and others like it. It's the perfect setting, nothing snobby or high-brow like the Christchurch galleries. It's got the right vibe. Or it will have with a little tweaking."

"Hm," said Maddy, taking an annoyingly long sip of

coffee, frowning at the table, lost in thought. "You are certainly the main attraction at the café. You know everyone and everyone knows you. That's why they go there. What about the food?"

"The chef wants to continue to work. She'll simply be working for me, with better wages.

"Are you sure you want to take on the responsibility of owning a café?"

Amber hesitated.

"You've never wanted it before," said Maddy. "In fact, you also seemed to hate any responsibility."

"That's true. But, you know, Maddy, I feel different since David came along. I mean, I know it's over between us—"

"Do you? I'm not so sure."

Amber gave Maddy a hard look. "It's over, believe me. How can I trust someone who wants to use me—someone who threw me a line and drew me in until he had me where he wanted me?"

"But he didn't use you, did he?"

Amber frowned. "What do you mean? Of course he did!"

Maddy leaned forward and put her hand over Amber's. "No, I mean, he intended to, I don't dispute that, but he didn't in the end, did he? I mean, he came clean and told you everything."

"And you think that's okay?"

Maddy pulled a face. "Not exactly, but–"

"No 'buts' about it! How can I ever trust him again?"

"Maybe by what his actions say about him, rather than his words? See what he does next. I've heard he's gone into business with Rob."

"Rob? Who told you that?"

"Gabe saw Rob last night."

"He didn't say anything to me!" Amber was annoyed that Rob hadn't thought to say anything to her about it.

"Maybe Rob doesn't know about you and David."

"Maybe," said Amber doubtfully. "But, even so. Why is David working with Rob? Rob is into heritage buildings."

"Maybe David has had a change of heart."

Before Amber could respond, the door burst open and Gabe planted a kiss on his wife's cheek, a pat on her stomach and grabbed a cup of coffee. "Amber!" He greeted her before downing half his coffee. He looked from one to the other. "What's going on? Have I missed something? You're both looking thoughtful, which is always dangerous."

Maddy grinned and gave Gabe a hug. "Sure is. Amber and I are going into business together."

Both Amber and Gabe looked up in surprise.

"We're going to buy the café. Amber's going to continue to do what she's so brilliant at—be the person who everyone comes to see and chat with—the village hub. And I'll do what I'm so 'brilliant' at." She tapped her laptop. "Create magic with my spreadsheets. I'll do the behind-the-scenes stuff and Amber will do the front of house stuff. It'll be a marriage made in heaven."

Gabe chucked her under her chin and kissed her. "That's what we have."

Amber groaned and took her empty cup to the sink. "I'm out of here. Thanks, Maddy. I think it'll be brilliant. Let's talk about it tomorrow." Amber plucked her bag from the chair and walked away from the kissing couple. "See you, then."

She didn't get a reply.

DAVID LOOKED around the packed museum. He saw Amber immediately, surrounded by her friends and family. His spirits dropped. He'd hoped he'd be able to exchange at least a few words with her, but knew that penetrating the force field that was her family would take more than his courage. But she'd see. Later, she'd see. She had to.

There was standing room only as the museum manager, wiping sweat from his forehead, squeezed through to the rear of the museum.

"As you can see," he said, indicating the donation indicator on the wall behind him, "our donations are down and we're going to have to reduce hours, as well as the pieces we show, if we are to continue at all."

There were murmurs of discontent and a few calls, including one from Jim Connelly. The museum director held up his hand for silence.

"Please, let me finish. We are simply under-funded and the council refuses to help us any more, which means we'll have to rely on the generosity of our community." There were more grumbles.

Jim cleared his throat. "As much as we appreciate the work the museum is doing, and its importance, we can't go on shoveling money into something which is a bottomless pit!" Jim's voice carried easily; his love for amateur dramatics always came to the fore at such public meetings. Other people muttered in agreement.

"There's only so much volunteers can do!" someone added.

"Exactly!" continued Jim. "Which is why we've cast our net a bit wider this time, and, hopefully, come up with a solution." The murmurs of discontent became friendlier. "I'll let David Tremayne outline his proposal."

The crowd parted and David stepped up to the small podium upon which the museum director stood, and for the first time in his life he felt a fluttering of nerves as he looked around. He was accustomed to public speaking, and he was used to telling people what to do. What he wasn't familiar with was imparting information, which was neither an instruction nor a command. He cleared his throat and glanced at Amber. He needed grounding, and he needed to be the man of whom Amber would be proud.

"We have a problem and I would like to propose a solution." Some things didn't change. He'd always appreciated clarity in public speaking.

"'We'? You don't even live here! We don't need some property developer coming in, tearing down our houses and donating money to assuage your conscience!"

Pandemonium erupted, which David tried to ignore as the museum director called for order.

"Mr. Tremayne *does* live here. Isn't that right?"

David nodded. "I live next door. I'm not going anywhere," he said, looking at Amber. The message was for her. "I'm here to stay. It's where my heart is."

For one long moment their gazes tangled before she looked away with an effort which David couldn't interpret. Did she understand what he was saying? Because, if she wouldn't take his calls, or talk to him directly, it was the only way he could get the message across.

"The old Granary?" asked Jim Connelly.

"That's right. And before you ask, I fully intend to restore it to its original glory. It'll complete the French quarter."

"And bring more attention to the museum," the museum director added.

"And I don't intend to donate any money."

Silence fell. "David," said Jim. "Why don't you tell us exactly what you do propose?"

"I happen to own one of the buildings in Christchurch, which has been re-designated as a house of special interest. I have full tenancy promised on that and I propose that a percentage of income received from the tenants be made over to the museum on a permanent basis."

"How permanent is permanent?"

David looked directly at Jim. It was obvious no one, except Jim and the museum director, believed him. And why should they? "Very permanent. I've had the papers drawn up already."

The museum director picked them off the table before him and raised them in the air. "Here they are—in black and white. An ongoing income which will both preserve the quarter, the museum, and allow us to enlarge our collection. It makes it a going concern, not just a concern," he said with a wry smile.

The mood turned and David soon found himself at the center of an excited group, explaining how his proposal would work. He left the museum director outlining what this would mean for the community in practical terms and went in search of Amber. She was talking to Maddy—an archaeologist with a passion for the place—who was even more excited than the others.

David had avoided Amber all evening. Now when he looked, she was too far away. If he went to her, it would be obvious. He turned to look at one of the exhibits, pretending to read it, when all his thoughts were on one person—the one person no one wanted him near. Only when the room was silent did he look around. But he wasn't alone.

"That's good of you, David," said Amber, who stood, red hair aglow in the evening light, her rainbow dress made of some silky stuff that shimmered around her. "To pledge money for the museum's upkeep."

He opened his mouth to speak but his vision was full of her and his self-discipline was fully employed in stopping him from reaching out to her and pressing his lips against hers. He shrugged instead. "It's the least I could do."

She cocked her head to one side. "The least?"

"I made a mistake, Amber. And I intend to put it right.

And what better way than to give to the very thing I wanted to rob the country of—its history?"

"But you did it to save lives. Zoe told me all about what happened."

"Right. Despite the fact I asked her not to."

Amber grinned. "It seems all the women in your life are unruly, not doing what you want them to do."

He shrugged and smiled back. "Perhaps it's for the best."

"Yes, I think you'll have to accept," she said, stepping closer to him, "that sometimes women know better than you."

He looked down at her, her sweet lips curved and infinitely kissable. He tightened his hands into fists in his trouser pockets, determined not to ruin the moment.

"I meant what I said back there, Amber. I'm here to stay. I know there's nothing I can say which will enable you to trust me again, and I don't expect it. But I can *do* something. I can live my life in a different way, with different values. And that's down to you."

"David, I…" He held up his hand to prevent her from taking a step closer. He didn't think he'd be able to stop himself.

"No, please. You don't have to say anything." He moved away.

"But I—"

He couldn't bear to hear her tell him that, despite everything, she still didn't trust him. He didn't know what he'd do if she said that. He walked quickly out the door without looking back, without saying goodbye, without listening to another word. He didn't notice the museum director who tried to talk to him, or Jim who was waiting for Amber, or anyone else who tried to speak to him. He just kept on walking. Because that was all he could do. Keep on walking, keep on showing Amber with everything that he did that he'd changed, that he could be trusted... especially with her heart.

~

AMBER ADJUSTED one of her paintings and turned at the jingle of the café door bell, a smile ready to greet her customer. *Her* customer. The smile froze as she saw who'd entered.

They'd been open a whole week already, but David hadn't come in, despite invitations from Gabe. And Amber had had to work hard at Gabe to make him pass on an invitation to David. Gabe reckoned he didn't want to be some kind of Eros go-between, but her wish had prevailed. It was never hard to make Gabe do what she wanted.

And here he was. He didn't look over at her, although he must have seen her upon entering the café. Instead, he greeted Gabe and Maddy at their usual table, and walked on to the table where he'd always used to sit.

"I'll get this," she said to the new waitress. Amber whispered a few quick instructions to the waitress, picked up the pen and paper and walked over to the table where David was looking at the menu intently. She cleared her throat. "Good morning."

He looked up. "It's afternoon."

She smiled. "Ah, so it is. You have me there. Good afternoon, then."

He smiled back. "Yes, I think it *is* going to be a good afternoon."

Her smile widened. Not even a polite 'hello' was simple with this man. She kind of liked the way he meant the words literally. That seriousness had always got to her. She cleared her throat, willing herself not to get distracted. "So, what can I get you?"

He looked back down at the menu. "Are the bread rolls

fresh?"

"David, they're always fresh."

"Ah, yes. I'll have the salad."

"Dressing to one side? Hold the coriander?"

He nodded, and she moved to one side to allow the waitress, to whom she'd just whispered the order, to place it on the table. After the waitress left, Amber leaned in and straightened his knife and fork.

"Am I really that predictable?" he asked, looking at the salad before him—dressing to one side, and a distinct lack of coriander.

"Yes," she said with a grin. "About your food, anyway. From what I hear, it's about the only thing that has stayed the same." She paused. "I'm glad. I wouldn't want everything about you to change."

He leaned back in his chair, his eyes never leaving hers. "Would you not? And what would you like to remain the same? My urbane charm?"

"You're not the charming sort."

His face fell. "What then?"

She moved into the seat opposite him, and reached out for his hand, slipping her fingers between his before gripping his hand. She lifted their joined fists between them. "The way your hand holds mine. Kind of possessive, but still I like it."

He squeezed her hand, and the sensation traveled all over her body.

"What else?"

"I like your seriousness. You take time over everything you do and give it your utmost consideration. You give everything one hundred percent."

"Of course."

"Not everyone does, you know. But most of all, I like the way you look at me. As if you want to make me yours but don't quite like to."

He looked surprised. "That about sums it up." He paused and looked at her. "And what about you? It's been a month since I last saw you. The café looks amazing; your art looks amazing, you—"

"Fine!" she exclaimed before he could say something which would totally annihilate her. "I'm fine. Some of my pieces have even been bought by someone who isn't you, would you believe?"

"I would. I haven't got any more room on my walls, anyway. Your paintings are everywhere in my house."

"Yeah, right," said Amber, not believing him. After all, he only bought her paintings because he felt sorry for her, right? "I'd like to see that." Her comment was meant to be sarcastic, but David took it seriously. Of course he did.

"Then come to my house. This afternoon, after work."

"Well, I…" She was confronted with what she'd been imagining since she'd last spoken to him at the museum. Of being alone with him. She was suddenly nervous. She'd spent many happy hours imagining that he really had changed, that he really did still have feelings for her. "I'm not sure."

His smile slipped. "Why aren't you sure?"

She shrugged. How could she tell him that she was scared that she'd find that, although everything appeared to be changing for the best, nothing had changed underneath it all? And that she was back to square one. A vulnerable woman, being used by a sophisticated man. She shrugged a second time.

He pulled her hand to his lips and kissed it lightly. "Amber, come to my house this afternoon and I'll show you what I've been doing."

"Okay," she said, her mouth apparently not obeying her brain. "I'll meet you at your house at four."

. . .

IN THE END, it was five o'clock before she left the café. She could have left earlier, but there was always some reason to put off the hour, something to delay getting her heart broken. What if he simply wanted to show off what he was doing? Okay, so he'd had a change of mind, but had he had a change of heart, too? She had no idea what he felt for her anymore. But she had a feeling she'd know by the end of the afternoon, and that was what scared the heck out of her.

Eventually, she could delay no longer, and found herself walking up the narrow path which led to his house from the road. It was a spectacular location, raised above the road and built on a shelf of land above which gardens rose to the top of the ridge. She paused and looked at it. It seemed to hover above the museum. She'd seen him painting. She'd caught sight of him sawing, and seen him up on the roof, hammering iron. She'd never seen any other tradesman there. Only David.

David came out of the house and stood beside her. "So, what do you think?"

"I think it's amazing."

"I've done it all."

"Yes, I know. What I don't know is why. Was it for some sort of penance?"

"No!" His brows scrunched. "Well, maybe. I don't know. All I knew was that I needed to get my hands dirty and to bring something wonderful to life again by myself."

She nodded. "You're transferring your energies into the building. That's good."

She could see from his expression that he didn't buy what she was saying, but he didn't say anything. "It *was* good. I'm just about finished."

Before entering the front door, they went out onto the deck which overlooked the whole of Akaroa, its harbor and, in the distance, Belendroit.

"Wow! You can see everything from here." She leaned over. "Even my cottage." For a moment she wondered if he often came up here and looked down to see if her light was on. One high window in which she kept a small lamp—in memory of her mother—was visible from that angle. She looked away quickly, up into the sky, where dark clouds were gathering, her stomach fluttering absurdly at the thought. "It looks like rain," she said, her eyes fixed on the sky, hardly daring to look anywhere else.

He stood beside her, also looking up into the sky. It seemed it was the safest focus for them both. "It's been threatening for some time."

"Yeah," she agreed. "You can feel it in the air." Just as she spoke, there was a distant rumble of thunder. They both turned to each other at the same time.

"Amber!"

"David!" They spoke at the same time. "Sorry, what were you going to say?"

"I've left a space there, on the outside weatherboards."

She fingered the space. It was in a prominent position beneath the window, which looked out over the harbor. "Why? What's the space for?"

"Because I hoped you'd accept a commission to paint something for me."

"You want me to paint something on the outside of your house for you? Really? What exactly?"

"A rainbow," he said, his words softly spoken, his voice a caress. "Would you?"

She nodded. "I'd love to." It was the sign she'd been waiting for. She knew she'd recognize it when it happened. "Oh, David."

Just then it began to rain. David took off his jacket and threw it around Amber's shoulders. She heard a clatter as something fell from his pocket. She saw something gleam, and she bobbed down and picked it up. It was a ring. A large, beautiful amber set in ornate antique silver and surrounded with far more expensive diamonds, which made the whole thing sparkle, shedding rainbows over the decking area and low trees which edged it.

"Oh my goodness! It's beautiful." She twisted it around in the light.

"Do you like it?" he asked, sounding unsure and very unlike himself.

She looked up at him. "Of course I do. Who wouldn't? It's the most beautiful ring I've ever seen."

He nodded, took the ring from her fingers and held it out to her. "It's for you, if you'll have it, if you'll have me."

Tears sprung to her eyes, and she nodded. He pushed the ring on her finger and cradled her face in his hands.

"So, do you forgive me for being such an idiot?" He didn't seem to notice her head nod in agreement. "I know what I did was unforgivable, but I couldn't see anything other than a need to do whatever it took to destroy dangerous old houses. But now I can. Now, I can see *you*, and from now on everything I do will put you first. If you are central to my life, then I know I'm on the right path." He gripped her hands with an air of desperation. "Amber, I know I don't deserve you, but will you marry me? Please?"

Amber might not have been able to trust many things, but she could trust the passion in his eyes and she knew that he spoke from the heart.

"Yes, David, I will marry you, because you're the only person I want to share my life with, share my rainbows and magic with. The only person I want to give my heart to—it's yours to keep."

"To keep," he murmured. "I like the sound of that," he added with a grin, before claiming her lips with his.

EPILOGUE

Two years later...

"And this," said Amber, balancing Skye on her knee as she completed the rainbow with one last swoop of palest lemon, "is it!" She sat back and hugged Skye. "The last rainbow in the house."

"Dada, Dada, Dada," said eight-month-old Skye. It was all she said. Apparently everything and everybody was her Dada.

"Good girl," said Amber, kissing her gorgeous chubby cheek. Amber could tell that David didn't entirely agree with how Amber praised her children for whatever they did. She thought if it had been left to David, he'd have them on some kind of genius regimen. Lucky for her, it seemed that he was putty in her hands. Putty in her hands, but still steel in the hands of everyone else, their children excepted. "Now," she said, standing up and holding her red-headed daughter up in the air until she giggled. "Let's go and find your real Dada."

It didn't take long because Skye's twin brother, River, was usually easy to find. You simply followed the noise. This time the noise took them behind the beautiful old home to the brand new extension, connected by the clean, soaring lines of a modern roofline. She entered the large airy space and stepped into a different world—David's world. Because, despite their acceptance and respect for each other, there was no getting away from it, they were two different people. And so they'd decided to build this extension so David could work from home with state-of-the-art communications and an interior decor in which there were fewer rainbows.

"Dada!" shouted Skye. David turned around and beamed to see his little girl shouting his name, even though she shouted it at everyone. Amber handed Skye over to David's willing arms, despite the fact he had renovation plans spread all over his desk, and went to the window where River was bouncing in a frame.

Amber grinned and picked him out of the bouncer. "Our River must have one of the best views in the world for his bouncer." But River appeared ignorant of the honor and squawked indignantly. Amber ignored his frown and planted a big kiss on his cheek. River's frown instantly disappeared and he, too, giggled as Amber played a kissing game with him.

"Um," said David, "I like the look of that game. Will you play it with me later?"

Amber raised an eyebrow. "You shouldn't say things like that in front of the children."

"As much as I love our children, I doubt they have sufficient genius at eight months old to understand a word of what I've just said."

"But they'll understand the feelings, the intent."

"If they understand that, then they'll know exactly how much I love you."

"Oh," said Amber weakly. "That's all right then. Because love always has a good, positive vibe." She lifted River so that his face was on a level with hers and David's. "Hasn't it, River? You understand love, don't you?" River grunted and moved his feet up and down as if he wanted to go for a run and then threw himself backwards in Amber's arms.

David laughed. "I think all River understands is that he wants to be moving."

Amber set him down on the floor and River quickly crawled across the floor and pulled himself up at the window.

David, holding Skye, joined Amber and River at the window, and they watched as River slammed his hands against the window, grunting with glee.

"I don't understand why River is so physical."

"Because he's a boy."

"You're typecasting."

"Amber, what did River do with that doll you gave him?"

Amber shrugged. "Threw it out the window."

"I rest my case. Whereas, this little girl." He held up Skye, who gripped onto his nose and laughed. "Just wants to be around people, don't you, my darling girl?" Whether Skye understood the words, or simply understood the energy of the love which was palpable from David, she leaned in and gave him a wet kiss on that same nose.

They looked out at the lanterns of Lantern Bay blinking amid the swirl of trees on that winter day. Still alight for anyone who might need to come home. But, thought Amber, *she* no longer needed them. She glanced at David, gently brushing Skye's red hair down on her head, and kissed River who squawked once more. She no longer needed them because she was already home.

~

AFTERWORD

Dear Reader,

I always admire people like Amber who are true to themselves no matter what. It takes courage to do that. At the beginning of the book it seemed that David was the intractable one and that if anyone needed to change it would be Amber. But never underestimate a strong, creative woman who is true to her ideals and doesn't care what anyone thinks!

By the end of the book David has given her the courage to be even stronger. And he's learned from her and is prepared to upend his life to show her how his values have changed. Sigh… I love a happy ending, especially when it's hard won.

Now all I have to do is to get the extremely capable Flo together with the extremely sexy Rob. They had a big bust up before he left to travel overseas, but he's back now, and it doesn't look as if he's going to leave any time soon. Wish me luck! I hope to have *Yours Forever* published by mid 2022.

Happy reading!

Sophie

Interested in reading more about the Connelly family?

The Connelly saga first began with *Summer at the Lakehouse Café* which tells Lizzi and Pete's story. The Connelly stories continue as follows:

—Lantern Bay—
Yours to Give (Max & Laura)
Yours to Treasure (Rachel & Zane)
Yours to Cherish (Gabe & Maddy)
Yours to Keep (Amber & David)
Yours Forever (Rob & Flo)
Yours to Love (Cam & Charlotte)

Read on for an excerpt from *Yours Forever*

YOURS FOREVER

BOOK 5 OF LANTERN BAY—ROB & FLO

A second chance at love...

Ten years ago, Rob Connelly's mother died, and he turned to his girlfriend, Flo Pelletier, for love and emotional support which she hadn't been able to give him. So he'd looked elsewhere for comfort.

A one-night stand had turned into a commitment which had exiled him from both his home and his happiness. But now he's back and Flo doesn't want anything to do with him.

Rob's apparent rejection of Flo had only confirmed what she'd always felt at a fundamental level—she can't trust in love and can rely only on herself. From her hippy parents to her boyfriend, everyone she loves leaves her. So, what choice does she have but to keep her heart armor plated, and her affections solely focused on her home, friends and paying guests?

But with a house as shaky as her finances, Flo has no option but to accept Rob's offer to renovate the house to keep her business afloat. But will their relationship heal, or will it founder amid Flo's insecurities, Rob's new responsibilities and secrets which literally emerge out of the woodwork?

Excerpt

"Rob!" Flo said, annoyed that despite her wish to avoid her ex-boyfriend, there was a note of excitement in her voice. She immediately tamped it down. "What are *you* doing here?" She was pleased she sounded annoyed.

"Good to see you, too, Flo," said Rob with his usual low rumble. His voice had always got to her, its vibrations traveling deep inside of her, making a connection she no longer wanted. He was wearing a bushman's oiled jacket left open, with worn jeans and a black t-shirt underneath. He was broader, more muscled than he'd been when he'd left Flo and New Zealand all those years ago—a period of time which she thought of as forever. He was, not to put too fine a point on it, even sexier than before.

Flo forced herself to ignore her instinctive reaction, which was to jump into his arms and allow him to carry her off. She'd done that years before and look how that had ended. She couldn't even allow herself to give her usual warm welcome to visitors, because Rob was different. Rob was the man who'd hurt her beyond pain itself.

"I guess you're here to see your little sister?" One thing was certain, Rob wouldn't have come to see Flo. When they'd last met, she'd made it clear she wanted nothing to do with him.

"Yep. Mind if I come in?" He glanced up at the leaking roof through which rain now ran in thick, rope-like cords. "I would have come to the back door as usual, but the path by the beach is impassable now. You really should—"

"Get that seen to," she interrupted. "I know, and I will."

Flo opened the door wide, and he stepped into the hallway. She suddenly remembered how he used to call and see her and her grandmother, his tall frame filling the hallway in a way which neither she, nor her grandmother, had ever done. He had a presence, and she'd forgotten about it. The appearance of Amber in the hallway, all large eyes and ethereal beauty, brought her back to the present.

"Rob! What are you doing here?" asked Amber.

Rob shook his head. "Not you, too." He sighed. "I'm here because David asked me to come."

"David?"

"Yes, David. Your husband."

Amber looked like she'd recovered. "I know who David is! What's happened? Is everything all right?"

"He's fine. He's still in Shelter Springs." His usual kind voice replaced the cool tone he'd used with Flo. He'd always been close to his youngest sister, and he obviously wanted to reassure her. "He says to tell you that Aimee sends her love."

"Aw, I miss my darling niece. Like you must miss your—"

"But he asked if I'd pick you up," interrupted Rob quickly.

Flo frowned. Rob might be a cheating bastard to her, but

he was the kindest brother, and she'd never heard him inter-rupt Amber before. Not even when Amber was at her wackiest.

"What were you going to say, Amber?" asked Flo. "Rob might miss what?" Or who, she thought to herself.

Amber blushed and looked nervously at Rob. She shook her head.

"David reckoned you'd have walked to Flo's," continued Rob, as if Flo hadn't spoken. "And the storm is only going to worsen."

Amber smiled at the thought of her doting husband. "How come my husband knows so much about me?"

"I don't know," said Rob with a smile. "It's almost as if he loves you or something."

Amber beamed. "Yes, he does."

Flo's heart tweaked a little, and she looked away. So much love and none of it for her. "Well, you'd best get going then." She gave Amber a quick hug. "Thanks for coming and getting me started."

"I'll be back when I can. And Maddy and Gabe will, too. We'll all pitch in and help." Amber turned to her brother. "Won't we, Rob?"

Rob raised his eyebrow in question at Flo. "That's up to Flo."

Amber turned to Flo. "You *will* accept Rob's help, won't you?"

Flo shot Amber a dark look. Amber knew full well that Rob was the last person she'd accept help from. They both knew. "No. But thank you all the same," she added. She might hate the man who'd broken her heart so many years before, but she could be polite and grown up about it.

"Why not?" asked Amber.

Flo lost control of the tumult of emotions which surged through her whenever Rob was around. "Because I don't want him around." Her heart pounded, and she regretted the words as soon as they'd escaped, like steam, relieving the pressure but scalding everyone in sight.

Rob sucked in a sharp breath. "Right, I guess that's our cue to leave. Amber? You ready?"

Amber was looking worriedly from Flo to Rob and then back to Flo again.

Rob sighed and disappeared outside onto the porch.

Amber ignored Rob's question and gave Flo a hug and held on tight. "I'm sorry," she whispered.

"It's okay. I shouldn't have said that, but I feel you guys are pressuring me to do something I don't want. Amber, after what happened, I don't want anything from your brother."

"I just want the people I love to love each other."

"That only happens in fairy tales."

"No, no, it doesn't. I won't believe it. I won't *let* it be like that."

"Please, Amber, just leave me be. I know what I'm doing." And right there was the biggest lie of all.

While Amber went to collect her things, Flo was drawn to the porch, her eyes fixed on the dark shape of Rob's back. She knew the tilt of his head, knew that her words had hurt him. And she felt guilty, despite the pain which she still nurtured and kept close—because how else could she protect herself?

"I'm sorry, Rob. That came out harsher than I meant it to."

His shoulders relaxed a little, and he turned slightly and looked over his shoulder at her. The dim yellow light of the outside light caught his face. It made his gaze warmer some-how. She swallowed.

"It's OK. I only hope that one day you'll forgive me."

Amber's arrival on the porch, carrying too many bags, saved Flo from answering. Amber juggled the bags as she tried to pull on her raincoat. Flo avoided Rob's eyes, but could feel his gaze on her as if it were a physical thing. It had always been like that. Some things, it seemed, never changed.

Amber yelped as a drip turned into a river of water as it broke through the rust in the porch roof. Was it Flo's imagination or was there more rain gushing through the holes in the porch? Amber put up her umbrella and grinned at Flo. "I'll be around again as soon as I can. But we've made a start." She gripped Flo's arm. "And don't forget to look for the key for the—"

A tearing sound from above interrupted Amber. Rob and Amber looked up. With one quick movement, Rob pushed Amber back into the hall, where she stumbled into Flo's arms as the porch roof came crashing down along with a waterfall of rain.

Without a thought, Flo rushed out into the pouring rain and grabbed Rob's arm as he threw aside a rusting piece of corrugated iron, which had narrowly missed his head. He pointed to it, his eyes ablaze.

"Are you OK?" shouted Flo above the sound of the thundering rain. She could hardly see him in the gloom, as the porch light had gone the same way as the roof. All she could see were angry eyes and rain-slicked hair and body.

"Amber could have been killed, Flo! Amber or you! This has got to stop right now!"

She released her grip on his arm and stepped away. "I guess you *are* OK."

"Come in, you two!" shouted Amber from the hall. "You're both going to get soaked."

"Too late for that," said Flo, relieved to release Rob's angry gaze and step back into the house. She busied herself, taking off her over-shirt and tossing it into the tray meant for umbrellas. She kept her gaze averted for a moment as she tried to slow her pounding heart. Rob was right, but she'd be damned if she'd admit it. Suddenly, she felt the tight grip of Rob's hand on her shoulder.

"Don't turn away from me again, Flo. This time it's serious. This place is a death trap, and it's about time you did something about it."

She lifted her chin angrily. "Don't you think I'm trying?" She took his hand and pulled it from her shoulder. "Don't you think I work every moment of every day to earn money to keep me, my house, my garden afloat?"

"It's sinking now," murmured Amber after peering out at the soggy lawn. She shot Flo an apologetic look. But Flo's gaze was firmly on Rob, who held up his hand to pacify her.

"Don't you hold up your hand to me, Robert Connelly, as if I'm some kind of mad dog that needs calming down!"

"He's only trying to help, Flo," said Amber, looking anxiously from one to the other. Flo sighed, exasperated. She knew Amber hated scenes, especially scenes between people she loved. Which meant virtually everyone in Amber's world.

"I know, but I don't need help." She turned away because she didn't want either of them to see she was lying or to see that her eyes were filled with tears. She waited for one of them to contradict the lie. But neither said anything. It was up to her. She looked up to the ornate plaster ceiling and blinked, willing the tears to disappear. She'd read somewhere that you couldn't cry if you looked up. She turned to them slowly and gave them a weak, rueful smile.

"Perhaps it would be more accurate to say I don't *want* help."

"No one wants help, Flo," said Rob, in a deep soothing voice which made a small place, deep inside of her, melt a little. "But sometimes you have to take it. You give to people all the time. It's about time you accepted something from them."

Damn. She couldn't stop her lips from trembling. She

didn't trust herself to speak. All she could do was nod, as she thought about all the work which needed doing on the house.

She sniffed and cleared her throat. "Well, I guess the porch…" she trailed off as her voice threatened to break.

"The porch, yes," said Amber, gamely poking her head out the open door. "That would be an excellent start. Very good indeed. Yes." She nodded, over-keen to get this scene over and move things onto a pleasanter footing.

Flo couldn't help smiling, understanding exactly what Amber was doing, and caught Rob's answering smile. "It would be a good start," she said to Rob.

For a moment, that little place inside of her which had melted at his voice, melted a little more under the tender gaze of his eyes. Then Amber moved, and the spell was broken.

"Brilliant!" said Amber.

Rob looked from Amber to Flo once more. "I'll be back in the morning to assess the damage. We'll have it fixed in no time."

"But I can't—"

"I don't want money. Actually, you'll be doing me a favor. I have skilled men waiting to begin work on a project in Christchurch. They can work here until the next project is ready."

He stepped away and turned to look outside. "Let's get going, Amber. I'll see you tomorrow, Flo. Bright and early."

"Right," Flo said. "And thank you!" she called out to Rob and Amber's receding backs as they ran across the soggy lawn toward the front gate where Rob's four-wheel drive was waiting. Rob waved a hand in acknowledgement before opening the gate for Amber.

Flo watched them leave. Then she glanced across at where she'd seen the man earlier and briefly wondered whether he'd been looking at her—it had certainly appeared that he'd been looking at the house—or whether it was a random moment. Random, she decided as her gaze turned up to the open sky where once the porch roof had been. The entire structure had twisted off its steel supports.

Rob had been right. It could have been very serious if he hadn't pushed Amber out of the way. She shuddered at the thought of Amber being hurt. She would never have forgiven herself. And if Rob had been standing slightly to the left... She closed her eyes with a gasp as she felt the pain which he would have felt. It sliced inside her and in that moment she knew she'd never be free of Rob Connelly. Whether she liked it or not, and she didn't, he occupied a place in her heart which would be forever his.

But that didn't mean she'd risk the pain of rejection again. Guilt motivated Rob—that much was clear. If he'd left her once for another woman, he could do it again. And that would kill her.

Bright and early, she thought, as she gave one last sweeping glance around the garden, being hammered by the rain. In the meantime, she thought, as she closed the door on the rain, she had work to do. She had guests to feed, rooms to clean, baking to do for the café. And then there was the decorating, the accounts, potting the plants she sold at the weekend market—the list was endless. She felt as if she were treading water with one arm tied behind her back and she was slowly—inch by inch—slipping under.

Bright and early, she repeated Rob's words. Despite her initial determination to keep Rob Connelly out of her life, she felt relieved. Maybe, just maybe, he'd just thrown her a lifeline.

Find out more!

ALSO BY SOPHIE HAYDON

The Mackenzies

A Place Called Home

Secrets at Parata Bay

Escape to Shelter Springs

What you See in the Stars

Second Chance at Whisper Creek

Summer at the Lakehouse Café

Lantern Bay